Richard Malcolm Johnston

Georgia Sketches

Containing : Mr. Israel Meadows and his School ; Judge Mike and his

Court...

Richard Malcolm Johnston

Georgia Sketches
Containing : Mr. Israel Meadows and his School ; Judge Mike and his Court...

ISBN/EAN: 9783337090814

Printed in Europe, USA, Canada, Australia, Japan

Cover: Foto ©Andreas Hilbeck / pixelio.de

More available books at **www.hansebooks.com**

PREFACE.

I have written these Sketches for the sake of the entertainment there was in thus employing some of the time in which I had nothing else to do. I am now going to publish them, because I trust they will impart to others, assuredly not the same amount, but enough to have me excused, both for the writing and for the publishing. I am willing that this be thought an apology instead of a preface; and if it be not a sufficient one, it is as great, I insist, as a man at my time of life ought to be expected to make.   C. P.

P. S.   I trust that those who have had either of the first two of these stories, (the former in Porter's Spirit of the Times, the latter in the Field and Fireside,) will not seriously object to see them again and in this present form

A GEORGIA SCHOOL IN THE OLD TIMES.

CHAPTER I.

"You call this education, do you not?
Why 'tis the forced march of a herd of bullocks
Before a shouting drover."

Books !—There is nothing terrible in this simple word. On the contrary, it is a most harmless word. It suggests quiet and contemplation , and though it be true, that books do often produce agitations in the minds of men and in the state of society itself—sometimes even effecting great revolutions—yet, the simple enunciation of the word, it would seem, could never be adequate to the production of even the smallest amount of excitement. As little would it seem, in looking upon it from any point of view into which one could get one's self, to be capable of allaying excitement and producing the most sudden and perfect stillness. I never could exactly tell why it is, that as often as I have read of the custom in England, of reading the Riot Act, during the progress of a riot, and begun to wonder how such an exercise was available in quelling it, my mind has recurred to the incidents about to be narrated, and been made at last, however reluctantly, to admit that the reading of the Act aforesaid, might be as proper a thing as could be done on such an occasion. For there was one point of view, or rather a point of hearing, from which one could observe the above last mentioned phenomenon produced by the utterence of the word which begins this story, twice a day for five days in a week. It was the word of command with which Mr. Israel Meadows was wont to announce to the pupils of the Goosepond school-house, the opening of the school morning and afternoon.

The Goosepond was situated in one of the counties of Middle Georgia, on the edge of an old field, with original oak and hickory woods on three sides, and on the other a dense pine thicket.— Through this latter there lay a path which led to the school from a neighboring planter's house where Mr. Meadows boarded. The school-house itself, a rude hut built of logs, was about one hundred and twenty yards from this thicket, at the point where the path emerged from it.

One cold, frosty morning, near the close of November, about twenty boys and girls were assembled as usual at the Goosepond, waiting for the master. Some of both sexes were studying their lessons and some were playing—the boys at bull-pen, the girls at jumping the rope —but all of them, with one exception—those studying and those playing, the former, though, the most eagerly—were watching the mouth of the path at which the master was expected. Those studying were the most anxious. The players seemed to think the game worth the candle ; though the rope jumpers jumped with their faces toward the thicket ; the boys invariably ran to the corner nearest to it when they were about to throw the ball, and looking behind a moment, would instantly turn and throw it at his man in the opposite direction. The students, they walked to and fro before the door, all studying aloud, and apparently exhibiting the greatest anxiety to transfer the secrets of knowledge which the books contained into their little heads. There was one boy in particular whose eagerness for the acquisition of knowledge seemed to amount to a most violent passion. He was a raw-boned boy of fifteen years, with very light, coarse hair, and a freckled face. He wore a round-about and pants of worn walnut dyed homespun, an old scalskin cap and red brogans without socks. He had come up after all the others had gotten there. He lived three miles and a half from the school-house, and walked the way forth and back every day. He came up shivering and studying, performing both of these apparently inconsistent operations with great violence.

'Hallo, Brinkly!' shouted half a dozen boys. 'Got in in time this morning, eh? ha! ha! Why, you are too soon, my boy. He

won't be here for a quarter of an hour yet. Come and help us out
with the bull-pen. Now, look at him, got that eternal jography, and
actily a studyin it, and he nigh an in about friz. Put the book down
an go an warm yourself a bit, and come and take Bill Jones' place·
Its his day to make fires. Come, we've got the inses.'

This last was addressed by the 'one exception' above mentioned,
a large, well grown, square-shouldered boy, eighteen years old,
named Allen Thigpen. Brinkly Glisson paid no attention to the
invitation ; but came on up shivering and studying, and studying
and shivering ; and just as he passed Allen he announced the following proposition :

'A-an emp-pi-re is a c-c-ountry go-go overned by an e-emperor.'

'Now ordinarily, the announcement of this proposition, one would
think would be entirely incapable to excite any uncommon amount
of risibility. It contains a simple truth and expresses it in simple
terms. And yet, so it was, that Mr. Allen Thigpen burst into a roar
of laughter : and as if he understood that the proposition had been
submitted to him for ratification or denial, answered,

'Well, Brinkly, spozen it is. Who in the dickens said it were'nt ?
I didn't ; did you, Sam Pate ?'

'Do what?' asked Sam, pausing in the act of throwing the ball.

'Did you say that a empire want a—what Brinkly said it was ?'
'I didn't hear what Brinkly said it was.'

Allen strode up behind Brinkly and looking over his shoulder·
said slowly, 'A country governed by an emperor.'

'No, I never said nothin about it : and I don't know nothin about
it ; nur I don't keer nothin about it neither.' And away went the
ball, but Sam had thrown it too suddenly, after looking towards the
mouth of the path, and he missed his man.

Allen laughed exceedingly at this effort at humor. But Brinkly
did not even notice the interruption. He walked to and fro, and
shivered and studied. He bowed to the book ; he dug into it ; he
grated his teeth, not in anger, but in his eagerness to get what was
n it ; he tried to fasten it in his head, whether or not, by slightly

changing the words, and making them, as it were, his c
mand.

'An yempire.' said he fiercely, but not over loudly, 'i
ge-uverned by an ye-emperor.'

'And what is a ye-emperor, Brinkly?' asked Allen, and
again.

'Oh, Allen, please go away and let me alone. I al
You know Mr. Meadows will beat me if I don't get it ; you
loves to beat me any how. Do let me alone ; it sorter
come to me now.' And he went on shivering and stu
shiveringly announcing, among other things, that, 'an y
a ke-untry ge-uverned by an ye-emperor,' emphasising e
the pollysyllables in its turn ; sometimes stating the
slowly and cautiously, and rather interrogatively, as if h
to doubt it ; at others asserting it with a vehemance whi
it to be his settled conviction that it was true, and th
doubted it, knew nothing about the subject.

Allen Thigpen turned from him and walked to w
cheeked little fellow, of eight years, was sitting on a s
spelling book in his lap, and a pin in his right hand wi
dotted every fourth word, after reciting the following :

'Betsy Wiggins.

Heneritter Bangs.

'Mandy Grizzle.

'Mine !·(dot.)   A-l-i-g-h-t light—alight.

'Betsy Wiggins.

'Heneritter Bangs.

'Mandy Grizzle.

'Mine! d-c-l-i-g-h-t light—delight,' and so on.

I yi, my little Mr. Asa,' said Allen, 'and spozen Bet
misses her word, or Heneritter Bangs-hern, or Mandy
then who's goin to spell 'em' I want to know ? And
me,' continued Allen, placing his rough hand with j
on the child's head, 'What'll you give me not to tell
you've been gittin your own words ?'

'Oh, Allen, please don't.'

'What'll you give me?'

'Twenty chestnuts.' And the little fellow dived into his pockets, and, counting out twenty, handed them to Allen.

'Got any more?' asked Mr. Thigpen, cracking one with his teeth.'

'Oh, Allen, please don't take 'em all.'

'Out with 'em, you little word gitter. A boy that picks oût words aint liable to eat chestnusts.'

Asa disgorged to the last one. Allen ate one or two, looking quizically into the child's face, and then handed the rest back to him.

'Take your chestnuts, Asa Boatright, and eat 'em. If ever I git to be as feared of a human as you and Brinkly Glisson is of Iserl Meadows, drot my hide ef I don't believe I will commit sovicide on myself—yes, on myself, by cutting my own throat.

'Yes,' answered Asa, 'you can talk so because you are a big boy. and you know he's afraid of you. If you was as little as me, you would be as afraid of him as me. If I ever git a man'—the little fellow was about to continue whimpering, but suddenly checking himself, he took his pin and mumbled :

'Betsy Wiggins.

'Heneritter Bangs.

'Mandy Grizzle.

'Mine!' he resumed his interesting and ingenious occupation of dotting every fourth word. Brinkly had overheard Allen's taunt, and closing his book, after a pause of a few seconds, he walked straight up to him and said :

'Allen Thigpen, I am no more afraid of him than you are ; nor than I am of you. I aint waiting to git to be a man to pay him back for the beating he has given me. Do you think that's what makes me stand what I do? If you do, you are much mistaken. Allen, I'm trying all the time hard to keep down on mother's account. I've told her of some of his treatment to me, and that I wouldn't stand it ; and she s always crying and telling me she is so anxious for me to git an education, and that its my only chance ; and it does seem it would nigh and in about kill her if I was to loose it, that I have been trying all I could to git the lessons, and to keep from fighting him when he beats me; and I could git 'em if I had a chance. But the fact is, I aint got on far enough in reading to have been put in this jography : and he's just put me in it before I learned to read right, just to git out of mother the extra pay for jography : and I can't git it, and I haven't learnt anything since I have been put into it ; and, Allen Thigpen, I am not going to stand it much longer, nor I aint going to pay you chestnus not to tell him I said so neither.'

'Hooraw !' shouted Allen, 'Give me your hand, Brinkly In a lower tone he continued, 'By jingo, I thought it was in you. I seen you many a time when, thinks I to myself, it wouldn't take much to make Brinkly Glisson fight you, old fellow.' Then taking him a little way off, he whispered, 'you've stood enough already, and too much, too. my blood has biled many a time when he's been a beating you. Don't you stand it no longer. Ef he beats you again, pitch into him. Try to ride him from the ingoin. He can maul you I expect, but look at this,' and Allen raised his fist, about the size of a mallet.

Brinkly looked at the big fist and brawny arm, and smiled dismally.

'Books !' shouted a voice, and Mr. Israel Meadows emerged from the thicket with a handfull of hickory switches.

In an instant there was a rushing of boys and girls into the house- all except Allen, who took his time. Asa Boatright was the last of the others to get in. He had changed his position from the stump, and was walking, book in hand, apparently all-absorbed in its contents, though his eye was on the school-master, whose notice he was endeavoring to attract. Book in hand, he bowed and digged and dived, until, as the master drew near, he weariedly looked up and seeing him quite unexpectedly, gave one more profound dive into his book and darted into the house.

It was a rule at the Goosepond, that the scholars should all be in and at their seats when Mr. Meadows arrived. His wont was to shout 'Books' from the mouth of the path, then to walk with great rapidity to the house. Woe to the boy or girl who was ever too late, unless it happened to be Allen Thigpen. He had, some months before been heard to say that ding any sich rule, and he wasn't going to break his neck for Israel Meadows nor nobody else ; and so he was wont to take his time. If he got in behind the master, which frequently happened, that gentleman was kind enough not to notice it—an illustration of an exception to the good discipline of country school-masters, which was quite common in the times in which Mr. Meadows lived and flourished.

On this occasion, when Mr. Meadows saw Allen, knowing that the gait at which himself was walking would take him into the house before Allen would get in, he halted a little, and taking a step or two, stooped, and having untied one of his shoe strings, tied it again. While this operation was going on, Allen went in. Mr. Meadows rising immediately, struck into a brisk walk, as if to apologise for his delay, and then entered into the scene of his daily triumphs.

But before we begin the day's work, let us inquire who this Mr. Meadows was and whence he came.

CHAPTER II.

Mr. Israel Meadows was a man of thirty-five or forty years of age, five feet ten inches in height, with a lean figure, dark complexion, very black and shaggy hair and eyebrows, and a grim and forbidding expression of countenance. The occupation of training the youthful mind and leading it to the fountains of wisdom, as delightful and interesting as it is, was not in fact Mr. Meadows' choice, when, on arriving at manhoods estate, he looked around him for a career in which he might the most surely develope and advance his being in this life. Indeed, those who had been the witnesses of his youth and young manhood, and of the opportunities which he had been favored withal for getting instruction for himself, were no little surprised when they heard that in the county of ———, their old acquaintence had undertaken, and was in the actual prosecution of the profession of a school-master. About one hundred miles from the Goosepond, was the spot which had the honor of giving him birth. In a cottage on one of the roads leading to the city of Augusta, there had .

lived a couple who cultivated a farm, and traded with the wagoners
of those days, by bartering, for money and groceries, corn, fodder,
potatoes, and such like commodities It was a matter never fully
accountable how it was, that Mr. Timothy Meadows, during all
seasons, had corn to sell.   Drought or drench affected his crib alike
—that is, they did not affect it at all.   When a wagoner wished to
buy corn, Timothy Meadows generally, if not always, had a little to
spare.   People used to intimate sometimes that it was mighty curious
that some folks could always have corn to sell, while other folks
couldn't.   Such observations were made in reference to no individual
in particular, but were generally made by one farmer to another,
when perchance, they had just ridden by Mr. Meadows' house while
a wagoner's team was feeding at his camp.   To this respectable couple
there had been born only one offspring. a daughter.   Miss Clary
Meadows had lived to the age of twenty-four, and had never, within
the knowledge of any of the neighbors, had the first beau.   If to the
fact that her father's always having corn to sell, without his neighbors
knowing exactly how he came by it, had to a considerable extent
discouraged visiting between their families and his (though it must
be owned that this was not the fault of the Meadowses, who had repeatedly, in spite of their superior fortune, shown dispositions to
cultivate good neighborhood with all the families around) if to this
fact be added the further one, that Miss Clary was bony, and, in no
respect, possessed of charms likely to captivate a young gentleman
who had thoughts of marriage, it ought not to be very surprising
that she had, thus far, failed to secure a husband.   Nevertheless,
Miss Meadows was eminently affable when in the society of such
gentlemen of the wagoners who paid her the compliment to call
upon her in the house.   So that no person, however suspicious,
would have concluded from her manner on such occasions, that her
prolonged state of single blessedness was owing to any prejudice to
the opposite sex.

It is a remarkable thing—whether in physiology or psychology, I
do really not know—how often, not only the traits of character and
the lineaments of form in parents are inherited by their children, but

their very habits and ways, and even the good luck and bad luck of thei^r lives. We have seen how that Mr· Meadows was wont to have corn to sell at all seasons, while nobody ever knew how he got it. Strange and unaccountable as this was, it was not more strange and unaccountable than a fact which, about this period of Miss Clary's life, transpired in her fortunes. To make short a long matter, Miss Clary had a baby; and in reference to this same baby, as to how it came there, there has been no more definite information—yea, even to this day—than as to how three-fourths of the corn which Timothy Meadows sold, found its way into his crib.

Israel, the baby—another thing uncommon with children—took the name of his mother. The class of children of which he was an individual, are wont to have no names except such as they can acquire by reputation. Generally, we know, society gives to the young the names of their fathers ; and by good rights, Israel ought to have borne another name than Meadows. Yea, doubtless, he would have done so if it had ever been possible for him to have found his father, But if he ever went out upon that laudible and pious pursuit, it is certain that he failed in the prosecution of it. And so society, being no more successful than himself, pronounced him in legal terms *nullius filius*, which was asserting in so many words, that he never had a father, and considering Miss Clary as solely responsible for his coming into the world, it gave him her name after he got here.

There were many interesting occurrences in the early life of Israel which it would be foreign to the purpose of this history to relate. It is enough to say, that he grew up under the eye and training of his grandfather, and soon showed that some of the traits of that gentleman's character were in no danger of being lost to society by a failure of reproduction.

In process of time, Mr. and Mrs. Meadows were gathered to their fathers, and Miss Clary, yet unmarried, had become the proprietress of the cottage and the farm. Israel had the luck of the Meadowses to be always able to sell corn to the wagoners. But unluckily the secret which lay hidden in such profundity during the lifetime of his grandfather, of how this wonderful faculty existed, did about six months previous to the period when he was introduced to the reader, transpire—a circumstance which would induce one to suspect, in spite of the declaration of law in such case made and provided, that there was something in the blood of Israel which was not all Meadows.

One Saturday night, a company of the neighbors on patrol found a negro man issuing from the gate of Miss Meadows' yard with an empty meal bag. Having apprehended him, they had given him not more than a dozen stripes with a cowhide, before he confessed that he just carried the bag full of corn to Israel from his master's corn crib. The company immediately aroused him, informed him what the slave had confessed, and although he did most stoutly deny any and all manner of connection with the matter, they informed him that they should not leave the premises until they could go and get a search warrant from a neighboring magistrate, by which, as their spokesmen, a shrewd man, said, they could identify the corn. This was a ruse to bring him to terms. Seeing his uneasiness, they pushed on, and in a careless manner proposed, that if he would leave the neighborhood by the next Monday morning, they would forbear to prosecute him for this as well as many similar offences, his guilt of which they intimated [they had abundant proof to establish. Israel was caught; he reflected for a few moments, and then, still, however, asserting his innocence, but declaring that he did not wish to reside in a community where he was suspected of crime, he expressed his resolution to comply with their demand. He left the next day.— Leaving his mother, he set out to try his fortune elsewhere, intending that by the time the homestead could be disposed of, he would remove with her to the west. But determining not to be idle in the meantime, after wandering about for several days in search of employment, it suddenly occurred to him one night, after a day's travel, that he would endeavor to get a school for the remainder of the year.

Now, Israel's education had been somewhat neglected. Indeed, he had never been to school a day in his whole life. But he had at home, under the tuition of his mother, been taught reading and writing, and his grandfather had imparted to him some knowledge of arithmetic.

But Mr. Israel Meadows, although not a man of great learning, was a great way removed from being a fool. He had a considerable amount of the wisdom of this world, which comes to a man from other sources besides books. He was like many other men in one respect. He was not to be restrained from taking office by the consciousness of parts inadequate to the discharge of its duties. This is a species of delicacy which, of all others, is attended by fewer practical results. Generally the most it does, is to make its owner confess with modesty, his unfitness for the office, with a he 'had hoped some worthier and better man had been chosen,' and then take it. Israel wisely reflected, that with a majority of mankind, the only thing necessary to establish for oneself a reputation of fitness for office, is to run for it and to get into it. A wise reflection indeed ; acting on which, many men have become great in Georgia, and, I doubt not, elsewhere, with no other capital than the adroitness or the accident which placed them in office. He reflected further, and as wisely as before, that the office of a school-master in a country school was as little likely as any he could think of, to furnish an exception to the general rule. Thus in less than six weeks from the eventful Saturday night, with a list of school articles, which he had picked up in his travels, he had applied for and had obtained, and had opened the Goosepond school, and was professing to teach the children spelling, reading and writing, at the rate of a dollar a month ; and arithmetic and geography, at the advanced rate of a dollar and a half.

Such were some of Mr. Meadows' antecedents.

CHAPTER III.

It was the custom of the pupils of the Goosepond, as in most of the other country schools of those times, to study aloud. Whether the teachers thought that the mind could not act unless the tongue was agoing, or that the tongue agoing was the only evidence that the mind was acting, it never did appear. Such had been the custom, and Mr. Meadows did not aspire to be an innovator. It was his rule, however, that there should be perfect silence on his arrival, to give him an opportunity of saying or doing anything he might wish. This morning there did not seem to be anything on his mind which required to be lifted off. He, however, looked at Brinkly Glisson with some disappointment of expression. He had beaten him unmercifully the morning before, for not having gotten there in time, though the boy's excuse was that he had gone a mile out of his way on an errand for his mother. He looked at the boy as if he had expected to have some business with him, which now unexpectedly had to be postponed. He then looked around over the school and said :

'Go to studyin.'

It was plain, that in that house, Mr. Meadows had been in the habit of speaking but to command, and of commanding but to be obeyed. Instantaneously was heard then and there, that unintelligible tumult the almost invariable incident of the country schools of that generation. There were spellers and readers ; geographers and arithmeticians, all engaged in their several pursuits, in the most inexplicable confusion. Sometimes the spellers would have the heels of the others, and sometimes the readers. The geographers were always third, and the arithmeticians always behind. It was very plain to be seen that these last never would catch the others. The faster they added or subtracted, the oftener they had to rub out and commence anew. It was always but a short time before they found this to be the case, and so they generally concluded to adopt the maxim of the philosopher, of being slow in making haste. The geographers were a little faster, and a little louder. But the spellers and readers had it, I tell you. Each speller and each reader went through the whole gamut of sounds, from low up to high, and from high down to low again ; sometimes by regular ascension and descension, one note at a time, sounding what musicians call the chromatic intervals ; at other times, going up and coming down upon the perfect fifths only. Oh ! it was so refreshing to see the passionate eagerness which these urchins manifested for the acquisition of knowledge. To have sliced out about five seconds of that studying and put the words together, would have made a sentence somewhat like the following :

C-d-c- twice e-an c-three r-ding-i-two l-v-old. My seven vill times a-do-l-cru-i-l coin-g-f-is man o-six-h-nin-four ni-h-eight cat p-c-a-t-r ten c-light is ca-light i-light x tween-by-tions fix dc-a-bisel-cru-fa-cor-a-light-bisel-rapt-double-fc-good ty-light man cra-forn-ncr-ci-spress-fix- Oh ! !'

To have heard them for the first time, one would have been reminded of the Apostles' preaching at Pentacost, and it might not have been difficult to have persuaded a stranger unused to such things that there were then and there spoken the languages of the Parthians and Medes, Elamites and the dwellers in Mesopotamia, and in Judea and Cappadocia; in Pontus and Asia; Phyrgia and Parophylia; in Egypt and in the parts of Syria about Cyrene; and strangers of Rome, Jews and Prossylites, Cretes and Arabians.— Sometimes these cloven tongues would subside a little, when it might be half a dozen would stop to blow; but in a moment more, the chorus would swell again in a new and livlier *ac crescendo.*— When this process had gone on for half an hour, Mr. Meadows lifted up his voice and shouted 'SILENCE,' and all was still.

Now were to commence the recitations, during which, perfect silence was required. For as great a help to study as this jargon was, Mr. Meadows found that it did not contribute any aid to the doing of his work.

He now performed a feat which he had never performed before in exactly that manner. He put his hand behind the lappel of his coat collar for a moment, and then, after withdrawing it and holding it up, his thumb and forefinger joined together, he said :

'There is too much fuss here. I'm going to drop this pin, and I shall whip every single one of you little boys that don't hear it when it falls. Thar !'

'I heerd it, Mr. Meadows. I heerd it, Mr. Meadows,' exclaimed simultaneously, five or six little fellows.

'Come up here, you little rascals; you are a liar !' said he to each one. 'I never drapped it; I never had nary one to drap. It just shows what liars you are. Set down and wait a while, I'll show you how to tell *me* lies '

The little liars slunk to their seats, and the recitations commenced. Memory was the only faculty of mind that underwent the
smallest development at this school. Whoever could say exactly
what the book said was adjudged to know his lessons. About half
of the pupils on this morning were successful. The other half were
found to be delinquent. Among these was Asa Boatright's class.
That calculating young gentleman knew his words and felt safe.
The class had spelled around three or four times, when, lo ! the
contingency which Allen Thigpen had suggested, did come to pass.
Betsy Wiggins missed her word ; Heneritter Bangs, (in the lan-
guage of Allen,) Lern, and Mandy Grizzle hern ; and thus responsibilities were suddenly cast upon Asa, which he was wholly unpre-
pared to meet, and which, from the look of mighty reproach which
he gave each of these young ladies, as she handed over to him her
word, he evidently thought it the height of injustice, that he should
have been called upon to meet. Mr. Meadows, closing the book,
tossed it to Asa, who, catching it as it was falling at his feet, turned,
and, his eyes swimming with tears, went back to his seat. As he
passed Allen Thigpen, the latter whispered :

'What did I tell you ? You heerd the pin drap, too.'

Now, Allen was in no plight to have given this taunt to Asa. He
had not given five minutes study to his arithmetic during the
whole morning. But Mr. Meadows made a rule (this one with himself, though all the pupils knew it better than any rule he had,) never
to allow Allen to miss a lesson ; and as he had kindly taken this
responsibility upon himself, Allen was wont to give himself no trouble about the matter.

Brinkly Glisson was the last to recite. Brinkly was no great
hand at pronunciation. He had been reading but a short time
when Mr. Meadows advanced him into geography, with the purpose, as Brinkly afterwards came to believe, of getting the half
dollar extra tuition. This morning he thought he knew his lesson ;
and he did, as he understood it. When called to recite, he went up
with a countenance expressive of wild happiness, handed the book
to Mr. Meadows, and putting his hands into his pockets, awaited the
questions. And now it was an interesting sight to see Mr. Meadows

smile as Brinkly talked of is-lands, and promonitaries, thismuses and hemispheries. The lad misunderstood that smile, and his heart was glad for the unexpected reception of a little complacency from the master. But he was not long in error.

'Is-lands, eh? Thismuses, eh? Take this book and see if you can find any is-lands, and promonitaries; and then bring them to me. I want to see them things, I do; find 'em if you please.'

Brinkly took the book, and it would have melted the heart of any other man than Israel Meadows to have seen the deep despair of his heart as he looked on it and was spelling over to himself the words as he came to them.

'Mr. Meadows,' he said, in pleading tones, 'I thought it was is-land. Here it is, I-s-l-a-n-d land : is-land ;' and he looked into his face beseechingly.

'Is-land, eh! Is-LAND! Now, thismuses, and promonitaries and hemispheries—'

Mr. Meadows, I did not know how to pronounce them words. I asked you how to pronounce 'em, and you wouldn't tell me; and I asked Allen, and he told me the way I said them.'

'I believe that to be a lie.'

Brinkly's face reddened, and his breathing was fast and hard. He looked at the master, as but once or twice before during the time he had looked at him, but made no answer. At that moment, Allen leaned carelessly on his desk, his elbows resting on it, and his chin on his hands, and said, dryly :

'Yes I did tell him so.'

Mr. Meadows now reddened a little. After a moment's pause however, he said :

'How often have I got to tell you not to ask any body but me how to pronounce words? That'll do, sir; sit down.'

Brinkly went to his seat, and looking gloomily towards the door a minute or two, he opened his book, but studied it no more.

CAAPTER IV.

Mr. Meadows now set about, what was the only really pleasant portion of his dutties, punishment of offenders. The lawyers tell us that of the several portions of the law, the *vindicatory* is the most important. This element of the Goosepond had been cultivated so much, that it had grown to become almost the only one which was consulted at all. As for the *declaratory*, and the *directory*, they were considered, when clearly understood, as impediments to a fair showing and proper development of the' vindicatory, in so much that the latter was often by their means, disappointed of a victim for its daily food. Mr. Meadows used to, somtimes when his urchins would not 'miss' or violate any law, to put the vindicatory first, punish an offender, and declare what he had done to be an offense, and then direct him that he had better not do so any more. He seemed to owe a grudge to society. Whether for its not having given him a father, as it had done to every body else, or because it had interfered in the peaceful occupation which he had inherited from his grandfather, as if to avenge itself on him for violating one of its express commands, that he, and such as he, should inherit nothing from aynbody, it did appear. But he owed it, and he delighted in paying it off by beating those children, each of whom did have, or had had a father. So, on this morning, by way of taking up another instalment on this immense debt, which, like most other debts, seemed as if it never would get fully paid, he took down his bundle of hickories from two pegs in one of the logs in the side of the house, on which he had placed them on his coming in, selected one five or six feet long, and walking to the middle of the vacant place between the fire-place and the rows of desks, he sat down in his chair and said :

'Them spolling classes and reading classes, and them others that's got to be whipped, all but Sam Pate 'and Asa Boatright, come to the circus.'

Five or six boys, and as many girls, from eight to thirteen years old came up, and sitting down on the front bench, which extended all along the length of the two rows of desks, and pulling off their shoes and stockings, the boys rolling up their pants, and the girls lifting their skirts up to their knees, they made a ring around Mr. Meadows as he sat in his chair, and commenced a brisk trot. They had described two or three revolutions, and Mr. Meadows was straightening his hickory, when Asa Boatright ran up, and crying piteously, said :

'Please sir, Mr. Meadows ; please sir, Mr. Meadows, let me go in the circus !'

Mr. Meadows rose up, and raised his hickory to strike ; but he looked at him a moment amusedly, and pointed to his seat. Asa went back to it, looking most forlorn. Mr. Meadows, resuming his seat, went at once into the exciting part of the exhibition, by tapping the legs as they trotted around him. This was done at first very gently, and almost lovingly. But gradually as the sport warmed in interest, the rapidity and violence of the blows increased. The children began to cry out, and then Mr. Meadows struck the harder, for it was a rule—oh, he was a mighty man for rules, this Mr. Meadows—that whoever cried the loudest should be hit the hardest. He kept up this interesting and exciting amusement, until he had given them about twenty five lashes apiece, the most of them being easily counted by the stripes. He then ceased. They stopped instantly, walked around him once, then seating themselves again on the bench, and resuming their shoes and stockings, they went to their seats. One girl, thirteen years old, had begged him to let her keep on her stockings ; but Mr. Meadows was too firm a disciplinarian to allow it. When she returned to the front bench, she put on her shoes, and taking her stockings up, and putting them under her apron, she went to her seat and sobbed as if her heart was broken.

Allen Thigpen looked at her a moment, and then he turned his eye slowly around and looked at Brinkly Glisson. The latter did not notice him. He sat with his hands in his pockets, and his lips compressed. Allen knew the struggle that was going on, and he longed to see how it would end. Mr. Meadows rested three minutes.

It has no doubt occurred to those who may have been reading this true story, that it was a strange thing in Asa Boatright, who so well knew Mr. Meadows; ways, that he should have expressed so decisive a wish to take part in this last described exhibition, an exhibition which, however entertaining to Mr. Meadows, as it doubtless was, and might be to many other persons, placing them in the attitudes of spectators purely, was not, to the highest degree, agreeable to one in the attitude which Master Asa must have known he would have been made to assume, had Mr. Meadows vouchsafed to have yielded to his request. But Asa was not a boy who was either a fool nor one who had no care for his physical well-being. He knew what he was about.

'Sam Pate and Asa Boatright,' said Mr. Meadows, after his rest come out here and go to horsin.'

The two lads came out. Master Pate gently inclined himself forward, an l Master Boatright got upon his back, and locked his arms around his neck. The former gathering the latter's legs in his arms, and drawing as tightly as possible his pants across his middle, commenced galloping as fast as he could around the area before the fire-place. Mr. Meadows having taken a fresh hickory, commenced appplying it with great force and precision to that part of Master Boatright's little body, which, in his present attitude, was the most exposed. Every application of this kind cpused that young gentleman to scream to the utmost of the strength of his voice, and even to kick, which, Master Pate being for the occasion a horse, was to understand as the expression of a wish on the part of his rider, that he should get on faster, and to frisk and to prance, and otherwise to imitate a horse as far as he could in the circumstances. Now, these circumstances being, that as soon as Master Boatright should have ridden him about long enough, to have become incapacitated from riding a real horse with even the smallest degree of comfort, they were to reverse positions, Master Boatright becoming horse and himself rider, they were hardly sufficient to make him entirely forget his identity in the personation of that quadruped. He did his best though in the circumstances, such as they were, and not only

pranced, but even neighed several times. When Asa was put into
the condition hinted at above, he was allowed to dismount. Sam
having mounted on his back, it was truly stirring to the feelings to
see the latter kick and the former prance. This was always the
best part of the show. A rule of this exercise was, that when the
rider should dismount and become the horse, he was to act well his
part, or be made to resume the part of rider, a prospect not at all
agreeable, each one decidedly preferring the part of the horse. Sam
was about three years older and twelve or fifteen pounds heavier
than Asa. Now, while Asa had every stimulus which as sensible a
horse as he was could have, to do his best, yet he was so sore, and
Sam was so heavy, that he met with much difficulty. He pranced
about furiously, but fell several times. Finding that he could do
no great things at prancing, he attempted to make up for this defi-
ciency by neighing. When Sam cried out and kicked, Asa neighed.
He would stumble against a desk and neigh; he would run head-
long against the wall and neigh; he would lift up one foot and
neigh; he would put it down, take up the other and neigh; and
then when he would attempt to lift up both feet at once, he would fall
down and neigh. Never before had Asa so well acted his part in
the horsin' at the Goosepond. Never before had horse, with such
odds on his back, neighed so lustily. Sam screamed and kicked·
Asa pranced and neighed, until at last, stumbling violently against
the bench, Sam let go his hold upon his neck, for fear of breaking
his own, and fell sprawling on his belly under a desk. Mr. Meadows
burst into a paroxysm of laughter. His soul was satisfied. He gave
up the pursuit and ordered them to their seats. They went to them
and sat down upon them with such a graduated declension of body,
as one would knowingly sit withal into a basket of eggs.

CHAPTER V.

After the close of the last performance which Mr. Meadows facetiously called 'horsin,' he rested about ten minutes. The most interesting, the most delightful, the most inspiriting exercise was yet
to follow. This was the punishment of Brinkly Glisson. It was

strange to see how he delighted in it. He was never so agreeable
at playtime, and in the afternoon, as when he had beaten Brinkly in
the morning. If he recited his lesson, and there was no other pre-
text to beat him, Mr. Meadows was sadder and more peevish than usual
during the remainder of the day, and looked and acted as a man who
felt that he was deeply injured. Now Brinkly was one of the best,
and bravest, and honestest boys in the world. He was the only son
of a widow, who had, at great sacrifice, sent him to Mr. Meadows'
school. He had pitched and tended the crop of a few acres around
her house, and she had secured the promise of a neighbor to help
her to gather it when ripe, and thus afforded her son an opportunity
of getting, as she said, a little schooling. He was the apple of her
eye—the idol of her heart. He was to her as we always think of
him of whom it is said, 'He is the only son of his mother, and she is
a widow.' The sacrifice she had to make, she made cheerfully : for
she loved him as she loved her own soul. And Brinkly had ever re-
paid that fond mother's care, by the most constant love and duty.
He soon learned to read tolerably at the school, and was advanced
into geography in a couple of months. How proud the widow was
when she bought the new geography and atlas, with the proceeds of
the sale of four pairs of socks, which (sweet labor of love !) she had
knit with her own hands. What a world of knowledge, she thought,
there must be in a book with five times as many pages as a spelling book, and in those great red, blue, and pink pictures, covering
a whole page a foot square, and all this knowledge to become the
property of Brinkly ! But Brinkly soon found that geography was
above his present capacity, and so told Mr. Meadows. That gentleman received the communication with displeasure ; said that
what was the matter with him was laziness, and that laziness, of all
the qualities which a boy had, was the one which he knew best what
   do with. He then took to beating him. Brinkly, after the first
eating, which was a light one, went home and told his mother of it,
and intimated his intention not to take another. The widow was
sorely distressed, and knew not what to do. On the one hand was
her grief to know her son was unjustly beaten, and his spirit cowed ;
or she knew that he studied all the time he had, and though unedu-

cated herself, she was not like many other parents of her day, who thought that the best means to develope the mind, was to beat the body. But, on the other hand, would be the disappointment of his getting an education if he should leave the school, there being then no other in the neighborhood. This, thought the poor woman, was the worse horn of the dilemma ; and so she wept, and begged him, as he loved her, to submit to Mr. Meadows. He should have the more time for study. She would chop the wood and feed the stock. He should have all the time at home to himself. He could get it, she knew he could. It would come to him after awhile.

Brinkly yielded ; but how many a hard struggle he made to continue that submission, no one knew but he,—not even his mother, for he concealed from her, as much as he could, the treatment which he had received and the suffering which he had endured. Mr. Meadows could see this struggle sometimes. He knew that the boy was not afraid of him. He saw it in his eye every time he beat him, and it was this which afforded him such a satisfaction to beat him. He wished to subdue him, and he had not succeeded. Brinkly would never beg nor weep. Mr. Meadows often thought he was on the point of resisting him ; but he knew the reason why he did not, and while he hated him for it, he trusted that it would last. Yet, he often doubted whether it would or not, and thus the matter became so intensely exciting, that he continually sought for opportunities of bringing it up. He loved to tempt him. He had no doubt but that he could easily manage him in an even combat ; but he did not wish it to come to that. He only gloried in goading him almost to resistance, and then seeing him yield.

Have we not all seen how the showman adapts himself to the different animals of the menagerie. How quickly and sharply he speaks to the lesser animals who jump over his wand and back, and over and back again, and then crouch in submission as he passes by. But when he goes to the lion, you can scarcely hear his low tones, as he commands him to rise and perform his part, and is not certain whether the king of the beasts will do as he is bidden or not. Doubts like these were in the mind of Mr. Meadows, when he was about to set upon Brinkly Glisson : but the greater these doubts, the more he enjoyed the trial. After a short rest from the fatigues of

the last exercise, during which he curiously and seriously eyed
the lad, he rose from his seat, paced slowly across the room
once or twice, and taking a hickory switch, the longest of all
he had, he stopped in the middle of the floor, and in a low
quiet tone, said :

'Brinkly Glisson, come.'

Allen had been eyeing Brinkly all the time, ' since the close
of the circus. He saw the conflict which was going on in his
soul, and when Mr. Meadows had burst into the paroxysm of
laughter, at the untoward ending of the horsin, he thought he
saw that the conflict was ended.

Slowly and calmly Brinkly rose from his seat, and walked
up and stood before Mr. Meadows.

'Why, hi!' thought Allen.

'Off with your coat, sir,'—low and gentle, and with a countenance almost smiling. Brinkly stood motionless. But he
had done so once or twice before, in similar circumstances,
and at length yielded. 'Off with it, sir,'—louder and not so
gentle. No motion on Brinkly's part, not even in his eyes,
which looked steadily into the master's, with a meaning which
he nearly but not quite understood.

'Aint you going to pull off that coat, sir?'

'What for?' asked Brinkly.

'What for, sir?'

'Yes, sir; what for?'

'Because I am going to give you this hickory, you impudent
scoundrel ; and if you don't pull it off this minute, I'll give
you sich a beatin' as'll make you feel like you never was
whipped before since you was born. Aint you going to pull
it off, sir?'

'No, sir.'

Allen wriggled on his seat, and his face shone as the full
moon. Mr. Meadows retreated a step, and holding his switch
two feet from the larger end, he raised that end to strike.

'Stop one minute, if you please.'

Mr. Meadows lowered his arm, and his face smiled a triumph. . This was the first time Brinkly had ever begged. He
chuckled. Allen looked disappointed.

'Stop, eh? I yi! This end looks heavy, does it? Well, I
would'nt be surprised if it war'nt sorter heavy. Will you pull
off your coat now, sir?'

'Mr. Meadows, I asked you to stop, because I wanted to say a few words to you. You have beat me and beat me, worse than you ought to beat a dog,' (Allen's face getting right again;) and God in heaven knows that, in the time that I have come to school to you, I have tried as hard as a boy ever did, to please you and get my lessons. I can't understand that geography, and I aint been reading long enough to understand it. I have asked you to let me quit. Mother has asked you. You would'nt do it; but beat me, and beat me, and beat me, (there is no telling whether Allen wants to laugh or to cry), and now, the more I study it, the more I don't understand it. I would have quit school long ago, but mother was so anxious for me to learn, and made me come. And now, I have took off my coat to you the last time.' (Ah! now there is a great tear in Allen's eye,' 'Listen to me,' (as the teacher's hand makes a slight motion,) 'don't strike me. I know I'm not learning anything, and your beating aint going to make me learn any faster. If you are determined to keep me in this geography, and to beat me, just say so, and I'll take my hat and books and go home. I'd like to not come to-day, but I thought I knew my lesson. Now, I say again, don't, for God's sake, don't strike me.' And he raised up both his hands, pale and trembling.

It would be impossible to describe the surprise and rage expressed on the face of Mr. Meadows during the delivery, and at the close of this little harangue. He looked at the boy a moment. His countenance expressed the deepest sadness; but there was nothing in it like disdance or threatening. It was simply sad and beseeching. The master raised his switch and struck with all his might across his shoulders.

'My God!' cried the boy; but in an instant sadness and beseeching passed from his face. The long pent up resentment of his soul gushed forth, and the fury of a demon glared from his eyes. He was preparing to spring upon Mr. Meadows, when the latter, by a sudden rush, caught him and thrust him backward over the front bench. They both tumbled on the floor, between the rows of desks, Mr. Meadows uppermost.

'It's come,' said Allen, quietly, as he rose and looked down upon the combatants.

Mr. Meadows attempted to disengage himself and rise; but Brinkly would rise with him. After several attempts at this,

Brinkly managed to get upon one knee, and by a violent jerk, to bring Mr. Meadows down upon the floor, where they were, in the phraseology of the wrestling ring, cross and pile. Mr. Meadows shouted to two or three of the boys to hold Brinkly until he could rise. They rose to obey, but Allen, without saying a word, put out his hand before them, and motioning them to their seats, they resumed them. And now the contest set in for good. Mr. Meadows struggling to recover his advantage, and Brinkly to improve what he had gained. The former's right arm was thrown across the latter's neck, his right hand wound in and pulling violently his hair, while his left hand pressed against his breast. Brinkly's left leg was across Mr. Meadows' middle, and with his right against a stationary desk, his right arm bent and lying under him like a lizzard's, and his left in Mr. Meadows' shirt collar, he struggled to get uppermost. When Mr. Meadows' upper parts were rising, and about to rule the ascendant, Brinkly's lower parts would swell like a sea wave. Between these two the strife was even; and it was plain the matter would have to be settled by Mr. Meadows' lower parts and Brinkly's upper parts. Yet, when Brinkly would attempt to raise his head, that hand wound in his hair would instantly bring it back to the floor. When Mr. Meadows would attempt to disengage himself from underneath Brinkly's leg, that member, assisted by its brother from the desk, against which it was pressed, held it like the boa holds the bullock. Oh, Mr. Meadows! Mr. Meadows! You don't know the boy that grapples with you. You blow, Mr. Meadows! See! Blinkly blows not half so hard. Remember, you walk a mile to and from the school, and Brinkly seven, often running the first half. Besides, there is something in Brinkly's soul which will not let him tire. The remembrance of long continued wrongs, which cannot longer be borne; the long subdued but now inextinguishable desire of revenge; every hostile feeling but fear—all these are now dominant in that simple but heroic heart, and if you hope to conquer, you must fight as you never have fought before, and never may have to fight again.

Your right hand pulls less vigorously at the hair of Brinkly's ascending head. Look there! Brinkly's leg has moved an inch further across you! Wring and turst, Mr. Meadows, for right under that leg, if any where for you, is now the post of honor. Can't you draw out your left leg, and plant it

against the desk behind you, as Brinkly does with his right.
Alas! no. Brinkly has now made a hook of *his* left, and his
heel is pressing close in the cavity behind your knee. Ah!
that was an unlucky move for you then, Mr. Meadows, when
you let Brinkly's hair go, and thrust both of your hands at his
eyes. You must have done that in a passion. But you are
raking him some now, that is certain. But see there, now!
he has released his grasp at your shirt collar, and thrown his
left arm over you. Good morning to you now, Mr. Meadows!

In the instant that Mr. Meadows had released his hold upon
his hair, Brinkly, though he was being gouged terribly, released his hold upon his collar, threw his arm over his neck,
and pushing with all his might with his right leg against the
desk, and making a corresponding pull with his left, he succeeded in getting fully upon him; then, springing up quick as
lightning, as Mr. Meadows, panting, his eyes gleaming with
the fury of an enraged tigress, was attempting to rise, he dealt
him a blow in the face with his fist, which sent him back bleeding like a butchered beast. Once more the master attempted
to rise, and those who saw it will never forget that piteous
spectacle of rage, and shame, and pain, and fear. Once more
Brinkly struck him back. How that brave boy's face shone
out with those *gaudia certaminis*, which the brave always feel
when in the midst of an inevitable and righteous combat!
Springing upon his adversary again and seizing his arms and
pinioning them under his knees, he wound his hands in his
shaggy hair, and raising his head, thrust it down several times
with all his might against the floor.

'Spare me! for God's sake, spare me!' cried Mr. Meadows,
in tones never before heard from him in that house.

Brinkly stopped. 'Spare you,' he said, now panting himself. 'Yes! you who never spared anything that you could
hurt! Poor cruel coward! You loved to beat other people,
and gloried in seeing them suffering, and when they begged
you to spare them, you laughed—you did. And now, you are
beat yourself and whipped, you beg like a dog. Yes, and I
will spare you,' he continued, rising from him. 'It would be a
pity to beat any such a poor cowardly human as you are any
longer. Now go! and make them poor things there go to
horsin again, and cut 'em in two again; and then git in the
circus ring, and make them others, girls and all—yes, girls

and all—hold up their clothes and trot around you, and when
they cry like you, and beg you to spare 'em, do you laugh
again.'

He rose and turned away from him. Gathering up his
books he went to the peg whereon his hat was hanging, and
was in the act of taking it down, when a sudden revulsion of
feeling came over him, and he sat down and wept.

Oh! the feelings in that poor boy's breast! The recollection
of the cruel wrongs which he had suffered; of the motives so
full of pious duty, which had made him endure them, the
thought of how mistaken had been the wish of his mother that
he should endure them; and then of how terribly they had
been avenged. These all meeting at once in his gentle but un-
taught spirit overcame it, and broke it into weeping.

Meanwhile other things were going on. Mr. Meadows, haggard, bruised, bleeding, covered with dirt, slank off towards
the fire-place, sat down in his chair, and buried his face in his
hands. The pupils had been in the highest states of alternate
alarm and astonishment. They were now all standing about
their seats, looking alternately at Blinkly and Mr. Meadows, but
at the latter mostly. Their countenance plainly indicated that
this was a sight which, in their minds, had never before been
vouchsafed to mortal vision. A schoolmaster whipped! beat!
choked! his head bumbed! and that by one of his pupils.
And that schoolmaster Mr. Meadows! Mr. Meadows, who,
ten minutes before, had been in the exercise of sovereign and
despotic authority. And then to hear him beg! A school-
master!—Mr. Meadows!—to hear him actually beg Brinkly
to spare him! These poor children actually began to feel not
only pity, but some resentment at what had been done. They
were terrified, and to some extent miserable at the sight of so
much power, so much authority, so much royalty dishonored
and laid low. Brinkly seemed to them to have transformed.
He was a murderer! a *regicide!!* Talk of the divine right of
kings. There was never more reverence felt for it than the
children in country schools felt for the kingly dignity of the
schoolmaster of forty years agone.

CHAPTER VI.

Allen Thigpen was the only one of the pupils who did not entirely lose his wits while the events of the last few minutes were transpiring. While the contest was even between the combatants, he stood gazing down upon them with the most intense interest. His body was bent down slightly, and his arms were extended in a semi circle, as if to exclude the rest of the world from a scene which he considered all his own. When Mr. Meadows called for quarters, Allen folded his arms across his breast, and to a tune, which was meant for 'Auld Lang Syne,' and which sounded indeed more like that than any other, he sang as he turned off, about half of the line beginning with

'Jerusalem, my happy home.'

When Mr. Meadows had taken his seat, he looked at him for a moment or two as if hesitating what to do. He then walked slowly to him and delivered the following oration :

'It's come to it at last, jest as I said. I seen it from the fust ; you ought to a seen it yourself, but you would'nt ur you could'nt, and I don't know which, and it makes no odds which, you did'nt. I did, and now its come, and sich a beatin, Jerusalem ! But don't you be too much took back by it. You war'nt goin to keep school here no longer to-day. nohow. Now, I had laid off in my mind to have gin you a duckin this very day ; and I'll tell you for why. Not as I've got anything particklar agin you, myself ; you have not said one word out of the way to me this whole term. But, in the fust place, its not my opinion, nor haint been for sometime, that you are fitten too be a schoolmaster. Thar's them sums in intrust—intrust is the very thing and the onliest thing I wanted to learn—I say, thar's them sums in intrust, which I can't work and which you can't show me how to work, or haint yit, though I've been cypherin in it now two months. And thar's Mely Jones, that's in the same, and she haint learnt 'em neither, and dinged if I believe all the fault's in me and her, and in course it can't be in the book. But that aint the main thing ; its your imposin disposi- tion. If this here school-house,' he continued, looking around, 'if this here school-house haint seen more unmerciful beatin than any other school-house in this country, then, I say its a pity that thar's any sich a thing as education. And if the way things has been car'd on in this here school-house, sense you've been in it is the onliest way of getting of a education, then I say again, its a pity thar's sich a thing. It aint worth while for me to name over all the ways you've had of tormentin o' these children. You know 'em ; I know 'em : every- body about this here school-house knows 'em. Now, as I said before, I had laid off to a gin you a duckin this very day, and this morning I was going to let Brinckly into it, tell I found that the time I seen was a comin in him was done come; and I knowed he would'nt jine in duckin you on account of his mother. Now I've been thinking o' this for more'n two weeks, bekase—now listen to me; did'nt you say you was from South Carolina?'

Pausing for, but not receiving an answer, he continued:

'Yes, that's what you said. Well, now I've hearn a man—a travelin man—who staid all night at our house on his way to Fluriday, say he knowed you. You aint from South Callina; I wish you was, but you aint; you're from Georgy, and I'm ashamed to say it. He ast me, seein me a studyin, who I went to school to, and when I told him, (Mr. Meadows appearing to be listening) Meadows,' says he, 'what Meadows?' 'Iserl' says I. 'Iserl Meadows a school-master, says he?' and he laughed, he did; he laughed fit to kill hisself. Well, he told me whar you was raised, and who you was. But you need'nt be too bad skeered. I aint told it to the fust human, and I aint going to tell you leave. Now, I had laid off, as I told you, to gin you a duckin, but I had'nt the heart to do it, and you in the fix you are now at the present. Nuff sed, as seed in a bar-room in Augusty on a piece of pasteboard, under the words 'No credit,' when I was thar. Wonder if thar's going to be much more schoolin here?'

Saying which, Allen puckered up his mouth as if for a whistle, and stalked back to his seat.

Mr. Meadows, during the last few sentences of this harangue, had exhibited evidence of a new emotion. When Allen told him what the traveler had said he looked up with a countenance full of terror, and on Allen assuring him that he had not mentioned it, he had again buried his face in his hands. When Allen went back to his seat, he rose and beckoning to him imploringly, they went out of the house together a few steps and stopped.

'I never done you any harm,' said Mr. Meadows.

'You never did, certin, thore,' answered Allen, 'nor no particklar good. But that's neither here nor thar; what do you want?'

'Don't tell what you heard tell I git away.'

'Did'nt I say I would'nt? But you must leave tolerble soon. I can't keep it long. I fairly eech to tell it now,'

The school-master stood a moment, turning his hat in his hands, as if hesitating what sort of leave to take. He timidly offered Allen his hand.

'I ruther not,' said Allen; and for the first time seemed a little embarrassed. Suddenly the man hauled his hat on his head, and walked away. He had just entered the path in the thicket, and turning unobserved, he paused, and looked back at the school-house. And oh, the anger, the impotent rage, the chagrin and shame which were depicted on his bloodshot face. No exiled monarch ever felt more grief and misery than he felt at that moment. He paused but for a moment. Then raising both his hands and shaking them towards the house without saying a word, he turned again and almost ran along the path.

After he had gone, and not until he had gotten out of sight, Allen, to whom all eyes were turned (except Brinkly's who yet sat with his head hidden in his hands on the bench) took Mr. Meadows' chair, and crossing his legs, said :

'Well, boys and gals, the Goosepond it seem are a broke up school. The school-master have, so to speak, absquatulated. Thar's to be no more horsin' here ; and the circus are clean shot up. And the only thing I hates about it is that its Brinkly that's done it and not me. But he would'nt give me a chance. No,' he continued, sorrowfully and as if speaking to himself, 'he would'nt give me a chance. Nary single word could I ever git him to say to me out of the way. I have misted lessons, 'deed I never said none. I never kept nary single rule in his school, and he would'nt say nothing to me.'

Then rising and going to Brinkly, he put his hand upon his shoulder.

'No, its jest as it ought to a bin ; you was the one to do it, and in the name of all that's jest, Brinkly Glisson, what *is* you been cryin about? Git up, boy and go and wash your face. I would rather have done what you've done, than to a bin the man that fooled the tory in the Revolutionary War, and stoled his horse in the life of Marion. Come along and wash that face and hands.'

And he almost dragged Brinkly to the pail, and poured water while he washed.

The children, recovering from their consternation into which they had been thrown by the combat and its result, now began to walk about the house, picking up their books and laying them down again. They would go to the door and look out towards Mr. Meadows' path, as if expecting and indeed, half-way hoping, half-way fearing that he would return ; and then they would stand around Allen and Brinkly, as the latter was washing and drying himself. But they spoke not a word. Suddenly Allen, mimicking the tone of Mr. Meadows, cried out :

'Asa Boatright and Sam Pate, go to horsin.'

In a moment they all burst into shouts of laughter. Asa mounted upon Sam's back, and Sam pranced about and neighed, ah, so gaily. Allen got a switch and made as if he would strike Asa, and that young gentleman for the first time in the performance of this interesting exercise, screamed with delight instead of pain.

'Let Asa be the school-master,' shouted Allen. 'Good morning, Mr. Boatright,' said he with meek humility. 'Mr. Boatright, may I go out?' asked timidly, half a dozen boys.

Asa dismounted, and seizing a hickory, he stood up in the middle of the floor, and the others formed the circus around him. Here they came and went, jumping over his switch, and crying out and stooping to rub their legs, and begging him to stop 'for God's sake, Mr. Boatright, stop.'

Suddenly an idea struck Mr. Boatright. Disbanding the circus, he cried out :

'You, Is'rl Meadows, come up here, sir. Been a fighteu, have you, sir ? come 'up. sir. Oh, here you are.'

Mr. Boatright fell upon the teacher's chair, and of all the floggings which a harmless piece of furniture ever did receive, that unlucky chair, did then and there receive the worst. Mr. Boatright called it names, he dragged it over the floor ; he threatened to burn it up ; he shook it violently ; he knocked it against the wall ; one of its rounds falling out, he beat it most unmercifully with that ; and at last, exhausted by the exercise and satisfied with his revenge he indignantly kicked it out of doors. amid the screams and shouts of his school-fellows.

CHAPTER VII.

'Far you well,' said Allen, solemnly, to the fallen chair.

They now all gathered u p their books and slates, and hats and bonnets, and started off for their several homes. Those who went the same way with Brinkly, listened with the most respectful attention as he talked with Allen on the way, and showed how bitterly he had suffered from the cruelty of Mr Meadows. They had already lost their resentment at the dishonor of that monarch's royalty, and were evidently regarding Brinkly with the devotion with which mankind always regard rebels who are successful. Each one strove to get the nearest him as he walked. One little fellow, after trying several times to slip in by his side, got ahead and walked backwards as he looked at Brinckly and listened. He was so far gone under the old regime that he felt no relief from what had happened. He had evidently not understood anything at all about it. He seemed to be trying to do so, and to make out for certain whether that was Brinkly or not. The voice of those young republicans, had Brinkly been ambitious, would have made him dictator of the Goosepond. Even Allen felt a consideration for Brinkly, which was altogether new. He had always expected that Brinkly would at some day resist the master, but he did not dream of the chivalrous spirit of the lad nor that the resistance when it should come, would be so terrible and disastrous. He had always regarded Brinkly as his inferior ; he was now quite satisfied to consider him as no more than his equal. How we all, brave men and cowards, do honor the brave !

And Brinkly had just given, in the opinion of his school-fellows, the most brilliant illustration of courage which the world had ever seen.

But Brinkly was not ambitious nor vain ; he felt no triumph in his victory. On the contrary, he was sad ; he wished it could have been avoided. He said to Allen that he wished he could have stood it a little longer.

'Name o' God, Brinkly Glisson, what for? It is the astonishenist thing I ever heerd of, for you to be sorry for maulin a rascal who beat you like a dog, and that for nothin. What for, I say again?'

'On mother's account.'

Allen stopped—they had gotten to the road that turned off to his home.

'You tell your mother that when she knows as much about that villian as I do, she will be proud of you for maulin him. Look here, Brinkly, I promised him I would'nt tell on him tell he had collected his schoolin account and was off

But you tell your mother that if she gets hurt with you for thrashin him, she will get worse hurt with herself when she knows what I do.'

Saying this, Allen shook hands with him and the others and went off, merrily singing 'Jerusa. n my happy home.' Soon all the rest had diverged by by-roads to their own homes, and Brinkly pursued his way alone.

It was about twelve o'clock when he reached home. The widow's house was a single log tenement with a small shed-room behind. A kitchen, a meat-house, a dairy, a crib with two stalls in the rear, one for the horse the other for the cow, were the out buildings. Homely and poor as this little homestead was, it wore an air of much neatness and comfort. The yard looked clean ; the floors, of both mansion and kitchen were clean, and the little dairy looked as if it knew it was clean, but that was nothing new or strange. Several large rose bushes stood on either side of the little gate, ranged along the yard paling. Two rows of pincks and narcissus hedged the walk from the gate to the door, where, on blocks of oak, rested two boxes of the geranium.

The widow was in the act of sitting down to her dinner, when hearing the gate open and shut, she advanced to the door to see who might be there. Slowly and sadly Brinkly advanced to the door.

'Lord have mercy upon my soul and body, Brinkly, what is the matter with you ? and what *have* you been a doing, and what *made* you come from the school. house this time o' day ?' was the greeting he met.

'Don't be scared, mother ; it is'nt much that's the matter with me. Let us sit down by the fire here, and I'll tell you all about it.'

They sat down, and the mother looked upon the son and the son upon the mother.

'I was afraid it would come to it, mother; God knows how I have tried to keep from doing what I have had to do at last.

'Brinkly, have you gone and fought with Mr. Meadows?'

'Yes, mother.'

'And so ruined yourself and me, too.'

'I hope not, mother.'

'Yes, here have I worked and denied myself; day and night I have pinched to give you an education, and this is the way you pay me for it,' and she fell straight to crying.

'Mother, do listen to me before you cry and fret any more. and I believe you will think I have not done wrong. Please, mother, listen to me,' he entreated as she continued to weep, and rocked herself in order, as it seemed, to give encouragement and keep time to her weeping. But she wept and rocked. Brinkly turned from her and seemed dogedly hopeless.

'Say on what you're going to say. Say on what you're going to say. If you've got anything to say, say it.

'I can't tell you anything while you keep crying so. Pleas* don't cry, mother. I don't believe you will blame me when I tell you what I have been through.' His manner was so humble and beseeching, that his mother not still and in a less fretful tone, again bade him go on.

'Mother, as I said before, God knows that I've tried to keep from it. and could not, you don't know, mother, how that man has treated me.'

'How has he treated you?' she inquired. looking at her son for the first time she had been sitting.

'You were so anxious for me to learn, and I was so anxious myself to learn, that I have never told you of hardly any of his treatment. Oh, mother, he has beat me worse than anybody ought to beat the meanest dog. He has called me and you poor, and made fun of us because we were poor. He has called me a scoundrel, a beggar, a fool. When I told him that you wanted me to quit geography, he said you was a fool and had a fool for a son. and that he had no doubt that my father was a fool before me.'

The widow dried her face with her handkerchief, settled herself in her chair and said :

'When he said them things he told a—what's not so ; I'll say it if he is a school-master.' And she looked as if she was aware that the responsibility of that bold observation was large.

'He said,' continued Brinkly, 'that I should study it, and if I did'nt git the lessons he'd beat me as long as he could find a hickory to beat me with. I stood it all because it was my only chance to git any schoolin. But I told him when

—that is when he called you a fool, and father one, too—that it was'nt so, and that he ought not to say so. Well, yesterday, you know you sent me by Mr. Norris' to pay back the meal we borrowed, and I did'nt get to the school-house quite in time. But he was'nt more than a hundred yards ahead of me, and when he saw me, he hurried just to keep me from being in time. When I told him how you had sent me by Mr. Norris', he only laughed and called me a liar, and then—look at my shoulder, mother.' .

He took off his coat, unbuttoned his shirt and exposed his shoulder and back, blackened with hideous bruises.

'Oh, my son, my poor son.' was all that mother could say.

She had not, in fact, know a tenth of the cruelties and insults which Brinkly had borne. He had frequently importuned her to let him quit the school. But she, supposed that it was because of the difficulties of learning his lessons which got for him an occasional punishment, and such as was incident to the life of every school-boy, bad and good, idle and industrious. These thoughts, coming with her ardent desire that he should have some learning, even at the cost of receiving some harsh and even unjust punishment, made her persist in keeping him there. Seeing her anxiety, and to avoid making her unhappy, Brinkly had concealed from her the greater part of the wrongs which he had suffered. But when she heard how he had been abused, and saw the stripes and bruises upon his body, her mother's heart could not restrain itself, and she wept sorely.

Well mother. I stood this too, but last night I could'nt sleep. I thought about all he had said and all he had done to me, and I made up my mind to quit him any how. But this morning before day I thought, for your sake, I would try it once more. So I got up and studied my lesson here and all the way to the school house; and I did know it, mother, or I thought I did, for he would'nt tell me how to pronounce the words, but Allen Thigpen did, and I pronounced them just like Allen told me. When I told him that, he called me a liar, and afterwards I begged him not to strike me but to let me go home. But would strike me, and I fought him.'

'And you done right. 'Oh, my son, my poor Brinkly! Yes, you are poor, the poor son of a poor widow ; but I am proud that you have got the heart to fight when you are abused and insulted. If 'd known half of what you have had to bear, you should have quit his school long ago, you should, Brinckly, my darling, that you should. But hew could you expect to fight him and not be beat to death ? Why didn't you run away from him and come to me? He would'nt have beat you so where I was.' And she looked as if she felt herself o be quite sufficient for the protection of her young.

'Mother, I did'nt want to run ; I could'nt run from such a man as he is. Once I thought I would take my hat and books and come away ; but I could not do that without running and I could'nt run ; you would'nt want me to run, would you, mother?' The widow looked puzzled.

'No, but he is so much bigger than you, that it would'nt a looked exactly like you was a coward ; and then he has hurt you so bad : my poor Brinkly— you don't know how your face is scratched.'

'I hurt him worse than he hurt me. mother '

'What?'

'I hurt him worse than he hurt me ; I got the best of it'.

'Glory!'

'In fact, I whipped him.'

'Glory ! glory !'

'When I had him down—'

'Brinkly, did you have him down, my son ?'

'Yes, and he begged me to spare him.'

'Glory be to—glory be to—but you did not do it, did you ?

'Yes, mother, as soon as he give up and begged me to stop, I let him alone.'

'I would'nt a done it, certin, shore !'

'Yes you would, mother ; if you had seen how he was hurt and how badly he looked, you would a spared him, I know you would.'

'Well, maybe I might ; I suppose it was right, as he was a man growed and a school-master to boot. Maybe it was best : maybe it was best—maybe I might a done it too.'

She had risen from the chair and was pacing the floor. This new view of Brinckly's relation to his tyrant was one on which she required time for reflection. She evidently felt, however, that as Brinkly had so often been at the bottom in the combat, now, when he had risen to the top, there was no great harm in staying there a little longer. 'But maybe it was best : I reckon now he won't be quite so brash with his other scholars.'

'He will never have another chance.'

'What ?'

'Allen has found out all about him, and where he came from, and says he is a man of bad character. He begged Allen not to say anything about it until he got his money and could git away. So he is quit and the school is broke up.'

'Glory ! glory ! hallelujah !' shouted again and sung the mother.

Let her shout and sing ! Infinite justice, pardon the poor widow for shouting and singing, now, when her only son, though poor and an orphan, though bruised and mangled, appears to her grand and beautiful as if he were a monarch's son and the heir to a mighty empire.

JUDGE MIKE AND HIS COURT

OR,

FIVE CHAPTERS OF A GEORGIA HISTORY.

———————•◂•◂•◂————————

CHAPTER I.

Once upon a time, in this glorious country, a respectable but uneducated gentlewoman, who had taken to her home the child of poor parents, had brought her up with much care and tenderness; and had, though reluctantly, allowed her to receive, at the hands of some other benevolent person, a year's schooling, had the misfortune to lose her protege. The young lady, who was very pretty, being offered a home in a family, where she supposed that she could find better society and more enjoyments than were to be had in the house of her first benefactress, accepted this offer, and refused to return. The good lady, in her distress, searching eagerly how she might avoid placing any blame upon the beloved child of her adoption, attributed her loss to education.

'It was education, sir,' she said bitterly, when she had given up her efforts to recover her lost love. 'It was education that done it all. They may say what they please about education: I do believe that the more education people have the meaner they get.' Woe had been to the schools and colleges henceforth if she could have had her way with them.

There are many persons in this, which, in our pride for some things she has done, we call the Empire State of the South, who feel and speak like this gentlewoman regarding another great instrument of civilization. A few of the judgments of our Supreme Court have appeared to them to be erroneous, and destined to be fruitful of evil effects upon the enjoyment of personal security and private property. Now if it be not, it ought to be generally known, that the judges of that Court are required, (and such has actually been the case with each one of them, that ceremony never having, in a single instance, been omitted,) to take solemn oaths on their accession to the Bench, that they will administer the laws of the State. Unfortunately, however, it has thus far, from some cause, been impossible for our Legislatures to make a perfect judiciary system. So various are the pursuits of men, so complicated are the relations of business and social intercourse, and so subtle are the influences, which control their minds and direct their actions, that our Legislators, even admitting that they have usually been our wisest and best men, have sometimes, as if to make good the saying, 'that there is nothing perfect under the sun,' enacted very unwise laws. These laws, our judges not being invested by the constitution with power to change them, have had occasions to declare to be in full force as long as they remain unrepealed. But many of those who have been dissatisfied with the judgments which seem so blameable, are wont, in their hasty indignation, to attribute all the consequences of erroneous legislation to the circumstances of there being an institution called 'A Supreme Court for the correction of Errors.' If we hear that, away down in a Wiregrass county, where there is not much of anything good to eat but beef, a hungry lout has stolen a yearling, and been acqutited on the trial of the indictment of a jury, the foreman of which had a hind quarter to himself, too cheap and asked no questions, why, there is the Supreme Court! Why don't it stop such things? If an evil disposed person is guilty of malicious mischief, or an owner of a tippling shop keeps it open on the Sabbath day, and a young solicitor, who has been six months or a year at the bar, does not know how to prosecute these offences, and they go unpunished. Why there now! didn't I tell you so? Can you expect anything else as long as we have a Supreme Court? If a good man's daughter, thirteen years old, is stolen, hurried before a Justice of the Peace, and in five minutes' time made the wife of a vagabond—good Heavens! Is there no law to prevent such outrages against the happiness of parents and the well being of society. None. Ah! no, I suppose not. That Supreme Court! it ought to be abolished. I do hope the next Legislature will abolish the whole concern. We shall never have any peace again until we get back to the good old times under which our fathers lived.

Well, those old times were very good in many respects. Beef was cheap, and the temptation to steal it was small. Men did not often commit malicious mischief, or keep open tippling houses on forbidden days, because land was not high, people lived more widely apart, and every one kept his own liquor at home, gave to his neighbor, and received from his neighbor as much as they wished ; and, except upon Sundays, when they went to church, all got drunk as often as they pleased. Nor did maids of thirteen very often run off with vagabonds; because, fortunately for themselves, they were kept at home with their mothers at that age, and knew no better than to obey them; while what few vagabonds there were, were wont, in the small developement which the credit system had undergone, to carry upon their persons the unmistakable badges of their profession.

It is pleasing to an old man, like me, to recur to those times. Corn, twenty cents a bushel, except to wagoners, who being strangers, and considering that their silver might prove to be pewter, were made to pay a quarter of a dollar. Bacon, no price at all, because everybody had a plenty, and because the woods were full of game, and the creeks were full of fish. Blessed be the memory of those old times ! The most of those who were then my friends and companions are gone, and I am left almost alone. But for the recollection of what they were to me, I say again, blessed be the memory of those old times!

But like all other times, they had their evils and their wants. Men and systems were not perfect even then. True, they had not many schools, and they had no Supreme Court. And yet, in what schools and courts they did have, there were many things, which, when men thought upon them at all, they thought might as well have been done differently, or left undone. The schools had ways of righting themselves. The things done in them, though seriously inconvenient at the time of their doing were not very serious in their consequences. Boys knew them to be, as they were, institutions too bad, to get used to them. Or, if asked down to a moderate and he got his ducking.

reasonable temperature. Not so with the Courts and the Judges, when, what sometimes was the case, one of the latter was neither fully educated in all the learning applicable to all cases arising in law and in Chancery, nor wholly above the prejudices and other infirmities to which the rest of mankind are subject.

While men are thinking of those old times, and reminding one another of the many glorious things which they had, (especially young men, who, having received them by tradition, regard them with peculiar love and veneration, I hope it will not be amiss in me—who have lived in both the old and the new —to describe as well as my memory will serve me, a character or two, and a scene or two, which the former enacted in a Court now nearly thirty years ago. And as I have used many words in the way of preliminaries, and as I have mentioned one fact which, (though it has nothing whatever to do with my narrative, except to help to illustrate its moral, is yet a fact, having transpired in the old times,) I will stop for a moment right where I am, and call what I have written a Chapter.

CHAPTER II.

A young man, a native of Virginia, and a graduate of the law-school in the University of that State, had come to Georgia for the purpose of seeking a home and practising his profession. One morning, in the beginning of spring, in company with a middle-aged gentleman, whose acquaintance he had newly made, he rode towards the village near which the latter resided, for the purpose of being introduced to some of the members of the Bar residing there. As the two were riding along, after some conversation upon the practice of law and other pursuits in the South, the younger gentleman asked of the elder if there was in the South a Court of Errors.

'I do not remember to have so heard, but I presume that you have such a Court.'

'Yes, indeed,' exclaimed the elder, 'many a one. We have no other sort in Georgia. But I know what you mean, sir,' he added, seeing the young man's surprise. 'I answered your question literally, because what I say is very nearly literally true, and it is so doubtless because we have no court for the correction of errors which those we do have continually commit. I know that I myself, although I once studied it, and was admitted to the Bar, practiced, and yet I have seen enough to know that, with our present judiciary system, the law can never become a science settled upon any ascertained principles.'

'There can be very little doubt as to that.'

'We have no lack of lawyers of real ability, but I doubt if there is in the South another State so deficient in its judiciary as ours. We have, as I said, many able lawyers, but seldom an able Judge. The salary is so small that a lawyer of first rate ability, unless he be a man of property, ('and such men,' he added, in parenthesis, with a slight touch of dignity which did not escape the other, 'rarely enter the professions,') will not go upon the Bench. It is, therefore, generally occupied by men of inferior learning and ability ; and as we have no Supreme Court, and each is independent in his circuit, there is of course no uniformity in their decisions, but many an error you may be sure. I reside here near the boundaries of three circuits. I and my neighbors of two adjoining counties, live under three different systems of laws. I am tolerably posted on that of my own circuit, but I dare not move out of it, as I have known others to do to their sorrow. Even here, whenever a new judge is elected, we shall have a new system to learn ; for, like every schoolmaster who begins by throwing out of the school-room all the text books which his predecessor employed, he will fear that he will be considered as nobody unless he overrules much of what our present judge has decided.'

'Does not your constitution provide for a Supreme Court ?'

'It does, but, bless you sir, the people are almost unanimously opposed to its being established. They say that they are already to much worried by Courts to think of making any more of them. The lawyers too, the most of them, are equally opposed to it, because they know—hang them, and who should know so well as they—that it would lessen litigation by lessening what is to them the glorious uncertainty of the law. A man who would get an office here must not open his mouth in favor of a Supreme Court. He had as well avow himself a disciple of Alexander Hamilton, or a friend of the administration of John Adams.'

They had just reached the public square and alighted, when Mr. Parkinson pointed to a little office on the corner of it, into which two men were entering.

'There go two limbs of the law now. We will go in at once.

and leading the way he walked in and introduced the young man, Mr. Overton, to Mr. Sandidge and Mr. Mobley.

Mr. Sandidge, ('Elam Sandidge, Attorney at Law,' Overton had read upon a shingle as he entered,) was about fifty years old; tall, with very long legs, which seemed as if they were ashamed of his rather short body, from the fact that they would never hold it straight up. He had long arms, long hands, and long fingers, which last never looked clean. He wore shabby clothes too, which, if they had been ever so fine, would yet have looked shabby for a habit he had of chewing tobacco all the time when he was not eating or asleep, and spitting on himself. Yet, for all these drawbacks, Mr. Sandidge had, as it seemed, an ambition to appear perfectly and universally agreeable. His countenance, when he looked at another, was invariably clothed in smiles. He never laughed, he only smiled. While nature had given him no very acute sense of the humorous ; and while, therefore, he never felt like laughing, he had, apparently from a sense of duty, learned to smile, and he smiled at everything. If one said 'good morning' to him, he was sure to smile as he returned the salutation. If one, in answer to an inquiry concerning his health, complained of a headache, he smiled the most cordial sympathy. There was no considerable amount of cheer conveyed by his smiles— no more than there was by his shabby coat and· hands; but like these they were a part of him, and one got used to them. But whoever said anything funny where he and others were standing, and no person laughed except Sandidge, who was sure to smile, he felt cut up.

When Mr. Parkinson introduced Mr. Overton, Mr. Sandidge arose and extended his hand with a smile, which seemed to say: 'Ah ! you young dog ! You have come at last ! I knew you would.'

Mr. Mobley was a stout, fine looking man, about twenty-three years of age, of the middle height, with dark complexion, very black hair and whiskers, and a fine mouth, full of large sound teeth of perfect whiteness. There was an ease and grace in his manner, and an expression upon his face which marked him at once to Mr. Overton as a well educated and talented man. Immediately after the introduction Mr. Sandidge looked at the new comers and then at Mr. Mobley with a smile, which the latter interpreted at once; and after an exchange of a few words of civility, he rose to go.

'No, do not leave, Mr. Mobley,' Mr. Parkinson said. 'We have no especial business with Mr. Sandidge, but came to see you both. So please to remain, unless you have business which calls you away presently.'

Mr. Sandidge smiles upon Mr. Mobley as he resumed his seat ; and but that we knew that he was bound to smile at all events, we should have suspected that he was infinitely amused by the idea that Mr. Mobley should have had any business of such pressing importance as to require him to go to it in a hurry. He then turned to Mr. Parkinson and smiled inquiringly, for this was the first time that that gentleman had ever called on him, except upon business.

'Mr. Overton has removed to Georgia with a view of becoming located permanently somewhere in the State in the practice of the law ; and I have brought him here to make him acquainted with you both, knowing that he could obtain from you more of such information as he needs than he could from myself; besides,' he added, looking at Mr. Mobley, 'I desired to give him an opportunity of extending his acquaintance among those with whom he might spend pleasantly such of his leisure as he will have when he is wearied with the dullness of Chesnut Grove.'

Mr. Mobley bowed : Mr. Parkinson rose, and saying that he would return in an hour, left the office, Mr. Sandidge smiling at him all the while, even at his back as he went out. A conversation was begun at once between the young men, with an occasional but rare contribution from Mr. Sandidge. The latter was no great talker in a social way. It was a wonderful thing to him how many things people could find to say to one another on matters of no business whatever, but only in the way of civility. He could talk forever on business, and in the Court house often made speeches of two hours length. He understood such things mighty well ; but it puzzled him to see two persons sitting down together and talking for hours on miscellaneous subjects, sporting from one to another with perfect ease, having no apparent motive except a desire in each to entertain the other. There was Mobley now, he would think, a young man, who in the Court house was as skittish as a girl, whose practice, though he had fine education and ability, after a year's pursuit of it, was barely supporting him, and yet, as soon as he was out of that dread place, and in the society of the most intelligent and able of the profession, he would bear

his part in the discussion of general subjects, and even of legal
questions. with an ease and fluency which made him the most
interesting of them all, and the object of the especial envy of
Mr. Sandidge.   Being no philosopher, Mr. Sandidge could not,
for the life of him, understand how these things could be ; and
it seemed to him to be not only strange, but wrong that Mr.
Mobley, whom he was accustomed to run over in the Court
house, should not only seem to be, but should actually be
above him everywhere else.   And yet such things have been
before and since, and are to be hereafter, and have excited the
surprise of others besides Mr. Sandidge.   How many young
men of excellent talents and the most finished education, have
for a year or two striven in vain to begin successfully careers
at the bar, and have at length shrunk from the pursuit, and
left its honors and emoluments to be gathered by the Sandidges !   The Sandidges whom men laughed at when they saw
them enter the profession, and whom they continued to laugh
at for half a dozen years, and after half a dozen more years
have carried them all their cases, and have at last lived to see
them rich and prosperous.   Mr. Sandidge would not have
thought of exchanging places with Mr. Mobley, or the fine
young fellow who had been just now introduced to him ; but
the more they ran on with each other about law, literature and
what not, the more he wandered at and envied what he thought
was their only gift.   But he smiled whenever anything was
said to him, or he was expected to say and did say anything to
them.   When Mr. Overton inquired if there was much litigation
in that circuit, and if money was to be made by the practice,
Mr. Mobley slightly blushed, looked at Mr. Sandidge, and answered that there was not a great amount of litigation then
originating, and that Mr. Sandidge knew more as to what was
to be made by the practice than himself.   Regaining instantly
his case of manner, he laughed good naturedly at himself, who
had managed, he said, 'thus far to make money to pay my
board and store accounts, and not, I think, anything over.   I
do not, however, despair to do better after a while,' he added,
looking composedly upon Mr. Sandidge.

Mr. Sandidge being thus appealed to, and looking as if he
felt that that was a subject of which he ought to know something, answered that there were some few lawyers in the circuit
who were making a living.   Law was a mighty hard thing to
make a living at.   He had been trying it twenty-five years

and better, and ought to know how hard it was. There was no business that it was not easier to make money at than law. If he had his time to go over again he hardly thought he would undertake it. Indeed, he knew he would not if he knew what a young man had to go through with the first five or six years. Now, Mr. Sandidge had commenced the practice of the law without a dollar, and with not even a good suit of clothes. But he economized. He borrowed money at eight per cent. and shaved paper at sixteen and twenty. He went to every Justices' Court in the county ; learned the name of every man in it, got acquainted with every man's business, hunted up and set agoing litigation, until here he was in the possession of at least forty thousand dollars. And though many a man would have shrunk from what Mr. Sandidge had to go through with, yet, Mr. Sandidge told a story when he said what he did. He would have gone through with it a thousand times over. For next to the money which he had made by the law, he loved the spyings which it gave opportunities to make into the secrets of his neighbors, their silent struggles with sufferings and embarrassments, and he loved yet more the influence which the knowledge thus acquired enabled him to exert over them. But it was not his wont to encourage young lawyers. Nobody encouraged him, he reflected, and let them encourage themselves.

'Yes,' he said, 'law is a hard thing to get on with. There's a power of books to read, which requires a power of money to buy ; and there are so many contrary decisions on the same pints, and the practice and the pleadings are so hard to learn, and then a man, a young man, has so often got to speak before the Court, where everybody is watching him, and when he don't know sometimes what to say, when a pint is made he did'nt expect, and aint prepared to meet, and he gets embarrassed, and sometimes even has to give up the case, and be non-suited. These things, as I said, and a heap of others I might mention, makes law a hard business to follow. But some men do, by hard labor, make a living by it, by being economical. They say in Alabama, and down in South-western Georgia, it is easier to get along with it, and that some men even make fortunes. There is more litigation there, and not so much competition. But,' he ended, smiling quite encouragingly, 'it may well stocked to be sure, but the more here. The profession is pretty ———— merrier, you know ;'

and he smiled almost audibly, and with such satisfaction at this attempt at pleasantry, that Mr. Mobley laughed at it heartily and said :

'And Sandidge, you know it is some consolation to a fellow who is getting along slowly to know that there are others who are at no faster pace than himself ; for appropos of your proverb is the one that misery loves company.'

'Just so,' answered Mr. Sandidge, and at this moment Mr. Parkinson returned, and the two took their leave.

When they were on their way home, Mr. Parkinson asked Overton how he liked the *specimens* as he termed his new acquaintances. The latter answered that he was much pleased with the young man.

And you are not very much pleased with Sandidge, I suppose ?

'Why, no, I cannot say that I am greatly prepossessed in his favor ; and I guess he returns the compliment, as he discourages my notion to practice law.'

'He does, does he ?' said Mr. Parkinson, laughing. 'I knew he would ; and though I am much of his opinion in regard to any young man who can do anything else, yet I must say that his example is encouraging. He very well illustrates how a man of little talent, and less education, can grow rich and even attain to some eminence at the bar. Sandidge is certainly a queer genius. Twenty-five years ago everybody laughed at him—the Judge, the lawyers, the juries, and the people. But Sandidge laughed too in his way, and worked every day and night ; and somehow he got into practice. The Judge and lawyers came at last to respect him, the sheriffs to fear him, and the people to be in awe of him, until now he has made a fortune, has more influence with the present Judge, and is more successful before juries than any lawyer in the circuit. I knew he would attempt to discourage you. He always does. I doubt if it is because he has no feeling, but because it gratifies his vanity to exaggerate those obstacles which he had to overcome, and which nobody thought he would. And Sandidge, though he looks like a fool, is really a pretty good lawyer. There are men infinitely his superiors, but he is untiringly industrious. He prepares his cases so thoroughly, and hangs to them so doggedly, and studies the people so constantly, that he is, I repeat it, the most successful practitioner I know. He loves the law ; he glories in it, and knows nothing outside of it.'

'But Mr. Mobley ; he is certainly a man of real talent and education. Is he not likely to succeed ?'

'Mobley has very superior talent and a most finished education. He was educated by an uncle who died during his collegiate life, leaving in the minds of his executors money to enable him to complete his course, and enter his profession. His parents both died when he was a child. But Mobley shines everywhere except in the Court room. There he does not yet seem to be quite at home. I have heard him speak once or twice, and he certainly speaks well. But Sandidge worries him so with the starting of unexpected issues that he is often put to his wit's end. If he could live without the practice, I am inclined to think that, notwithstanding his pride, he would abandon it. He will succeed though after a while, I doubt not, if he will persevere. He is a fellow of fine wit, and gores Sandidge badly sometimes when he can reach him, which is not often the case, with this weapon. But Sandidge only smiles, and almost always gives things a turn which is sure to give him the best of it at last.'

'Do you usually have much business in the Courts?'

'And if so, which of these men do I employ to attend to it, you would ask. Well,' continued Mr. Parkinson, somewhat apologetically, 'what little I have do in that way, I usually give to Sandidge. I have known him a long time, and he has always seemed to act an honest part towards me. Besides, a man, you know, does not usually like to change the channel of his business.'

Mr. Parkinson did not have the heart, after what he had said of Mr. Sandidge's influence with the presiding Judge, to give that as another reason for retaining him.

The young man said nothing; but he thought with himself that, hard as it was on a poor fellow like Mobley, it was natural. And is it the less hard because it is natural that the world will delay to give help to a man in any business of life until, by long toiling and striving alone, he has at last reached a point where he can live without it? Yet, such is the way of life. You men with many clients, and many more friends, has there not been a time when nineteen of every twenty of those whom you now value the most highly would have forborne to lend you a helping hand, but would have waited until they had seen whether by the aid of the few who did stand by you, you were likely to rise or to fall? Let us not then fall out with what is natural in our fellow men, and what our very selves would do, and what we actually do, because it is natural to us. We would spare ourselves many an uncomfortable feeling of contempt, for the infirmities of human nature as we see them illustrated in the lives of our neighbors, if we would but reflect that, what is more often than otherwise the case with us, we would act in the same circumstances just as they do. Ask yourself, O! best of men, how many young men are there in any profession whom you so cordially wish to prosper in it, that you would be willing to take any of your business out of its old tried channel—a channel so freighted with yours and other people's bus-

iness that it would not miss the little you take from it—and risk it
in their care until they have proved that the consignment will be a
safe one? Or if you sometimes do this, is it not done a little slyly, and
do you not feel like apologizing, and when discovered, do you not
actually apologize to the old channel, and tell how trifling was the
freight you have taken from it, and how you supposed it would not
care to be pestered with such a small matter? Yes, and the old
channel says it makes no difference, and that it is all right; but
then you feel as if it was not all right, and as if you had injured the
old channel, and you go to work straightway, and ship a whole
boat load on it at once.

CHAPTER III.

'Can't we get through with the docket by Friday night!'

'There's business enough here to occupy the whole week and more
too. You'll have to sit an adjourned term to get through with it.'

'I shall do no such thing; and what is more, I shall adjourn the
Court Friday night.'

Mr. Sandidge smiled with wonted complacency. 'I don't think
we can hardly get to the Appeal before Wednesday dinner; and it
looks like a pity but what some of them cases that's been continued
so long could be tried. We lawyers ain't like judges to go and
draw our salaries every three months, but have to wait until the
cases are disposed of, and sometimes a long time getting them
then.'

This excellent joke put him on a broad grin. The judge did not
seem to appreciate it much, though he smiled in faint commenda-
tion. He was fifty years old, twenty-five of which had been spent
in the practice of the law in which he had risen to a fourth rank.
As a set-off to this professional eminence, he had remained as he
had begun, poor in purse. Three years before this an election was
being held for the office of judge of the Superior Court of that circuit. Let us remember that at that time the judge of the Superior
Court was the only high judicial officer in the circuit. He was both
judge and chancellor. His discretion was uncontrolled and uncon-
trollable in all cases regarding the security, the property, and reputation of citizens; and even his construction of the Constitution of
the State was unalterable by any human power. Three years before, politics had taken one of its turns, and the party to which the
fourth-rate lawyer of twenty-five year's practice belonged, unexpectedly found itself with a small majority in the legislature. The in-
cumbent of the Bench, being a member of the minority, was of course
to share its fate and retire from office. There were two prominent candidates from the party in power; one a retired member of Congress
who was finding it difficult to recover the practice which he had
given up fifteen years before, and the other a man of ten years con-

nection with the profession, of very promising talents, and of a good property, who sought the office for the eclat, and the power which it would confer upon him. Several ballots had been made without an election. Mr. Elam Sandidge, for certain reasons of his own, had consented to represent his county in the Senate, and was one of the party in minority. A more amused man it was seldom any one's privilege to see than was he when on the repeated counting out of the votes the presiding officer announced that there had been no election. He looked to this and to that one on either side of the house, and went about whispering to some and winking at others.

'What is that dirty old rascal doing on our side of the aisle?' inquired a majority member of his neighbor.

'I can't tell ; but some rascality brings him here', you may swear to that.'

While the votes were being counted out for the fifth time, Mr. Sandidge walked quickly over to that side. A dozen anxious, pitiful looking members gathered around him.

'Put him up next ! put him up next time!' he said, and walked back again, taking in with a sweeping wink the whole of his own party. When the result was announced, and directions given to prepare for another balloting, 'Mr. President, Mr. President,' screamed a voice from the majority side, 'I announce the name of Littleberry W. Mike, Esq , from the county of ———. This announcement was followed by roars of laughter from the minority and by hisses, and cries of 'who is he ?' from the other. Immediately, however, the leaders of both were busy as bees. Threats and criminations were heard among the friends of the two prominent candidates; then entreaties from both to the opposition. 'Take him down, for Heaven's sake.' 'It is a shame by blood.' 'Don't put him on us, if you please.' 'Any body else,' &c. All to no purpose. The nominee was elected on the next ballot.

'Why, how did you get elected, Berry ?' slyly asked Mr. Sandidge of the judge elect, as on the dispersion of the members he met him, trembling and pale as a corpse, at the foot of the gallery, and shook his cold hand. 'It appears like you must have got some votes from our side of the house.' The newly elected pressed the hand of his friend, and they went together to the hotel, on the way to which he was forced to hear from among the crowd many a bitter jest of which he was the subject.

This election was an instance of that miserable policy yet adhered to, by which minorities, in order to render majorities odious, do not hesitate to contribute all they can to make them do the greatest amount of harm to public interests. Men may say what they will of caucuses, but until there is a higher standard of public and private virtue amongst us. they will be indispensable.

When a man of inferior parts is raised to an office of great authority, he is apt, unless he has great virtue, and very amiable dispositions, to exert that authority, as far as is compatible with safety, in enforcing a regard which those parts have been inadequate to secure. Cowardly as this is, it is not more injurious to truth, and justice, and reason, than when such a man is led by such an elevation to look upon himself as having been heretofore depreciated, and to consider the elevation, whatever were the circumstances which affected it, as the decree of infinite justice in his favor, determining at last to give merit its just reward. Sometimes he is in one, and sometimes in the other of these two states alternately ; never being able to determine exactly whether he ought to occupy his position or not, but ever attempting to resolve the doubt by such a vigorous exercise of authority as will at least foreclose all doubts in the minds of others as to his actual possession of it. Of such a character was the newly elected judge. He had long had his heart set upon the bench. He looked up to it as a mighty eminence—mighty enough to satisfy the most eager ambition. Yet his desires were not actuated wholly by ambition. He wanted the salary. He needed it. He was poor and had a family ; and pitiful as the salary was, it was twice as much as he made by his practice. Ashamed as he was to know how the people regarded the notion of his being Judge of the Superior Court, he never, even for one moment, gave up his desire to become so, but kept himself always, yet in a quiet way, in candidacy for it. And though to the leading members of the bar he had never presumed to speak of the matter, knowing that he would be laughed at if he did, they yet well knew what his thoughts and his hopes were. Nor had he publicly announced his candidacy at the meeting of the Legislature. He knew well that his only chance of election depended upon the fact, whether true or false, it made no material difference with him, that he was considered the weakest and shabbiest of the candidates of his party. While the prominent ones of these were making interest with the leaders of the party in the Legislature, he had quietly, and in a way known only to himself and them, and very probably to Mr. Sandidge, obtained the promise of assistance from a few unknown members who should be able, by scattering their votes under the direction of him and Mr. Sandidge, to defeat the election of any one until a suitable opportunity should occur for the name to be presented. We have seen with what result this was done.

With the recollection of all the circumstances, Judge Mike thanked two objects for his elevation : first, his own lucky genius, and secondly, Mr. Sandidge. He was, doubtless, quite inclined to indulge in kindly and grateful feeling towards the latter from habit ; for he was under a pecuniary indebtedness to him of several hundred dollars under a writ of fieri facias which Mr. Sandidge, three or four years before, had been kind enough to 'lift,' to have transferred to himself, and to forbear enforcing payment thereof in consideration of sixteen, which he called a living per centum of interest. What sacrifices the indulgent creditor was always making, when at every renewal of the note for the extra interest, he solemnly avowed his need of the money, and of his submission to go without it for no earthly reason than to oblige his friends! On that friend's accession to the Bench, when first they were alone together, he took the last note of renewal from his pocket book, and handed it to him without saying a word. The judge, appearing surprised, Mr. Sandidge, with smiling solemnity, protested that he never could exact usurious interest from a Judge of the Superior Court of the State of Georgia. He hoped he had too much respect for the dignity of the office to do any such thing as that. The judge, after feeble remonstration, took the note, looked at it, sighed, and tearing it slowly to pieces, felt already one of those palpitating and almost painful joys which only men in office have. It was a small matter, but it touched him, for his means were small, and he felt as if henceforth he could live.

But to return to the conversation with which this chapter began, and which took place in the judge's room at the hotel, on the Sunday night before the sitting of the court.

'How does that smart chap Mobley get on?'

'About like he was.'

'Knowing everything but law, I suppose, and knowing nothing about that?'

'Just so. The fellow studies like rip, but judge, he don't study right. He studies books instead of men.'

Mr. Sandidge delivered this sentiment with contemptuous pity.

'He thinks if we had a Supreme Court he would do something grand.'

'He's for a Supreme Court, is he?' inquired the Judge, with a frown.

'Warm, warm. Has been from the first.'

'It wi'l be some mo before he gets it I'm thinking.'

'That's what I tell him.'

'Thank God, it's only these book men that want a Supreme C nt. They don't know, Sandidge, they don't know anything outside of books.'

'Not the first thing. That's what I tell 'em.'

'They think that because such a pint has been decided such a way, by such a judge, that it should be decided so always; and they are forever and eternally talking about settling the law, settling the law—like it was, Sandidge—just like it was so much coffee.'

Mr. Sandidge spat all over himself, wiped his mouth with his hand, and came very near laughing outright.

'And I would like to know how, in the name of common sense, it ever could get settled. There aint any thing to settle it by. That's the pint; there aint any thing to settle it by.' He looked enquiring' at Mr. Sandidge, and seemed to wish that gentleman to tell what there was to settle it by if he knew of any such thing. The latter shook his head.

'No sir! there aint nothing to settle it by and when Mobley is talking about what Lord Mansfield said, and what Lord Hardwick said, or any of them old lords and judges, it's on the eud of my tongue to stop him, and tell him that they are all dead, and consequently can't know any thing about the case at bar. And, Sandidge, it always struck me as very curious that the laws of England should be the laws of Georgia'

It was a remarkable coincidence that that idea had over and over again struck Mr. Sandidge. He, however, hinted, that in some cases, (and those were cases in his opinion when the authority happened to be on his own side,) where the English law was very plain and directly in point, and it ought to be followed.'

'Certainly, certainly, in such cases: and I do follow it; but I am the judge of that myself.'

'Ah! yes—that was right! Now they were exactly agreed. The judge, if he was judge, of course, ought to be the judge. If he

wasn't, of course, he couldn't be, which was absurd ;' and Mr. Sandidge almost frowned in the effort of elaborating this *reductio ad*
absurdum.

'Absurd—so I think; and Mobley and such as he may study their eyes out
for me. When they bring up law that I think is right, I shall sustain them;
when I don't think so I shall overrule them. They may get their Supreme
Court if they can. It aint going to be in my day, thank God. If it was, I
just know that I couldn't and wouldn't stand it. Before I would have an
overseer over me, and I judge of the Superior Court, and have to be eternally
looking into old books to find out what them old English lords and judges
said a hundred years ago, when the country wasn't like this, nor the people
neither—why Sandidge you know I havn't got the books, and couldn't afford
to buy them—I say before I would be put to all the trouble and expense of
reading law and nothing else, and then have my decisions brought back on me,
and treated like I was—like I was in fact a nigger—I would die first.'

Mr. Sandidge smiled approvingly.

'Why, who would respect me ?'

'Nobody.'

'How could I enforce the authority of the Court ?'

'Couldn't be done.'

'If I put a fellow in jail just like as not they would take him out.'

'Like as not.'

'If I fined one, ten to one it wouldn't stick.'

'Just so. He wouldn't stay found.'

'If I refused to grant a new trial, knowing that I am against them, they
would send a paper ordering me to grant it. Don't you see they would
knowing I am against 'em ?'

'Plain as day. Send a paper ordering the Judge of the Superior Court !'

'I tell you, Sandidge, before I would stand it, I would die first. In fact, I
would RESIGN ! !'

This was capping the climax. Dying would be a poor and very inadequate resentment. He would go beyond that. He would voluntarily and
disgustedly let go his hold upon power. The consequences might be what
they pleased, he would resign. 'I tell you, Sandidge,' he repeated once more,
with fearful emphasis, 'I should RESIGN ! !'

Mr. Sandidge, although purposing to appear alarmed, smiled notwithstanding ; and perhaps the more because he thought such a deplorable event
not very likely to come to pass; and perhaps yet more, because it instantly
assured to him that if it ever should, he would console himself in the midst

of his own losses and grief as well as he could by replacing the extra interest upon the FI FA not yet paid off and discharged.

'And what will you leading lawyers do when young men, smart young men, like Mobley, go before the Supreme Court with books in their hands and turn you down?'

'I shan't live to see it,' and it was doubtless the prospect of a far distant organization of such a tribunal, rather than of his own early decease, which gave the gratified and complacent expression to that smiling countenance.

CHAPTER IV.

Overton attended the Court, and obtained, by the assistance of Mr. Mobley, a seat within the bar. He had been introduced to several lawyers from different counties within the circuit, and to the judge. On his introduction to the latter, he remarked a certain ungainly attempt at a congratulation on his expected accession to the profession, which was anything else but cordial. Mobley had spoken of him to the other lawyers, in the judge's hearing, as a young man of education and genius, when Mr. Sandidge, who was sitting by him at the time, whispered that that was the sort of men who were always talking about a Supreme Court. After this, His Honor took no further notice of him. During the week, he noticed what was new to him, how much of an art it was to conciliate and to control the Court. It was evident that Mr. Sandidge was the favorite. Every body knew that. Mr. Sandidge himself, who had long foreseen and fore-ordained it. Of all positions in a free government, where favoritism is worth having, it was that of a favorite circuit judge of Georgia in the old times. When the fortunes of men, their security, and sometimes even their lives were dependant upon the will of an individual, and that individual amenable to no earthly tribunal for whatever errors he might commit, or even for his wickedness, except upon principles the most vague and uncertain, it was an art ranking as high as the science of the law itself, and attainable by greater cost and sacrifice, to obtain an easy and successful access to the ear of that most important depository of power. They were the fortunate accidents of our ancient judiciary system, that there was a goodly number of virtuous and talented men upon the bench; for neither virtue nor any very considerable amount of talent were essential qualifications. If the occupant for the time being possessed them, very well. If not, then not so well, yet well enough.

The present occupant, we have seen, had no uncommon talents. In virtue, he was neither good nor bad. At least, he was incapable of bribery. If he was below the capacity to feel or to understand a noble impulse, he was above that of perpetrating an act of plain dishonesty. In talent and in virtue, he might be said to have occupied a middle state between high and low, but tending downwards. Fortunately for some, unfortunately for others, he was not brave. Now, of all official personages, cowards are the most troublesome and oppressive. They are troublesome to those of whom they are afraid, and oppressive to those who are afraid of them; troublesome to the former by inflicting petty annoyances, in the use of small advantages, and the punishment of unimportant lapses in remembrances, and in resentment of the pain they feel on account of such persons; oppressive to the latter in order to preserve the equilibrium between the feeling and the excitement of fear. This quality is not peculiar to official nor even to human cowards. Instance canine. I once saw in the city of Milledgeville, one cur badly bitten and conquered in single combat with another. Immediately afterwards, as with his tale shrunk between his hind legs, he was making for home with what speed he could employ, he spied one of those dogs commonly denominated amongst us as fice, whereupon his tail at once came out to its natural suspension; he rushed upon the little animal, and without any known justifiable cause, and even without any previous acquaintance with him, caught him by the throat and shook him until he was beaten off with rods. After he had gotten out of the reach of these, he went on his way leisurely, apparently satisfied that he was again even with the world.

Mr. Sandidge was the favorite. The judge liked him not only for past favors of the kind we know of, but for another reason. He thought Mr. Sandidge a man like himself and about his quality; and, therefore, he liked to do honor to himself as it were in honoring his image. Mr. Sandidge made no great pretension to a knowledge of books, and he thanked him for that. He never even hinted about a Supreme Court, but seemed to be, as in fact he was, satisfied with the way of the present administration of justice. Such being the relations between them, Mr. Sandidge was lucky in getting rulings in his favor. He was in fact a much better lawyer than the judge, and shrewd enough to beguile him of many a wrong decision, even had he been different to him.

But, notwithstanding this favoritism, there were two or three lawyers of real ability who, in spite of their contempt of him and his dislike of them, exercised over him that influence which a strong and bold intellect will always exert over a weak and timid one. Above flattering him, they often, and even against Mr. Sandidge, obtained rulings of doubtful right, when he was unable, out of his dread of their unconcealed contempt, to resist them. But to compensate Mr. Sandidge for such as this, and to preserve his own regard for himself, he eagerly sought for opportunities to help him in taking advantage of oversights in pleadings and in proof; oversights which Mr. Sandidge himself never committed. The latter was, in addition, graciously allowed to domineer to any extent over the younger lawyers. They stood in great awe of the bench. They could neither cajole nor browbeat. Even a respectful remonstrance from them was usually followed by a frown, or a threat of it. They, therefore, timidly went about their business in the Court, hoping for the coming of the day when they might be the browbeaters of Sandidges.

Like most small-minded men who go up on the bench, this judge set himself up for a great reformer of abuse. He was a terror to evil doers; especially to those who did it on a small scale. Whenever he got a chance he was wont to stick the law on to them (to use his own phrase) up to the very hilt. There were two vices in particular which he hated cordially. They were fighting and usury. Whenever he could get a blow at either of these, he struck it with all his official might. Mr. Sandidge well knew his weakness on the subject of usury, and managed so as to have no cases of his own, but confined his financial operations to shaving paper. And yet he was lucky enough to make more out of usurious transactions than he was accustomed to when he loaned out his own money. For now the pleading of usury had become common, and there was no lawyer who could compare with him in ferreting testimony to establish its proof.

Of the younger lawyers, Mr. Mobley was an exception so far as to the standing in any awe of the judge. He was usually very much embarrassed in the management of his cases, because of his apprehension of being cast by the starting of some unforeseen difficulty, as was often the case from the want of familiarity with precedent and form. Here was Mr. Sandidge's forte. He understood pleading and the rules of practice thoroughly, and it was his delight to pick flaws in his adversary's papers, and drive him out of court. Mr. Mobley was afraid of him on these grounds, and well he might be; but otherwise he was incapable to fear. For people were generally in great need of the court. Here was where he could domineer at his pleasure. They should feel his power. All absences of witnesses and jurors, all noises in the court room and court yard, all misdemeanors, all suits, met with ready and condign punishment; always the more condign when their convictions came on shortly after a series of browbeatings from those whom he could not frighten. One morning during the progress of a trial in which his patience had been sorely tried a man in the crowd near the bar having a cold blew his nose—an action natural and necessary to the preservation of whatever amount of comfort is consistent with that ailment. The action in this instance was accompanied by

the usual loudnesss of sound produced by those who have uncommonly good
lungs.

'Mr. Sheriff bring that nose-blower within the bar.'

The culprit was brought in.

'Is this court a stable, sir, that you must bray in it like a jackass?'

The unhappy man answered the question respectfully and candidly in the
negative.

'What do you bray in it for then, sir?'

'I did'nt br—. I did'nt know I was a brayin in it jedge. I only blowed
my nose, havin of a bad cold.'

'What are you doing here any way, sir?'

'I jest come to court, sir.'

'Got any business here?'

'No, sir.'

'What did you come for, then?'

'Why, I thought, jedge, that everybody was liable to come to court.'

'Liable, liable! yes, and so are they liable to behave themselves; and if
they don't, they are liable to be fined. What is your name, sir?'

'Allen Thigpen, sir.'

'Thigpen, Thigpen! I might have known that any body by that name
could'nt tell a court room from a stable. Mr. Thigpen you are fined in
the sum of two dollars.'

Mr. Thigpen ran his hand into his pocket, and drawing out a dirty buckskin
purse, emptied it, and counting the pieces with a rueful face, walked up two
or three of the steps, and extending his hand to the jedge. Dollar one-and-
nine is the highth of what I could raise if I was going to be hung.'

Now, whether from looking upwards at so resplendent a luminary as the
judge, or from the violence of his cold, we could not say; but, as His Honor
was gazing upon the extended hand in ludicrous surprise and wrath, Mr.
Thigpen felt a sudden impulse to sneeze—an impulse which, whenever it
comes, in court rooms or elsewhere, must be obeyed. He made herculean
efforts to suppress it; but as is usual in such cases, the victory was but the
more triumphant and violent. In his terror, and endeavoring to assure the
judge that he was doing his best, he could not avert his eyes from him. His
face assumed the agonized contortions of a maniac; his great chest heaved like
a mountain in labor, and he uttered a shriek which, in any circumstances but
those which showed that nothing serious or uncommon was the matter, would
have filled all within a circle of two hundred yards diameter with consternation.
In the violence of the paroxysm, the coin flew up from his hand as if they had

been discharged from a catapult, and coming down, some of them fell upon the judge's head and rolled into his lap. An instantaneous burst of laughter followed this explosion, which, however, was as instantly hushed. No words can depict the expressions upon the faces of the two prominent actors. The judge had been, as it were lifted out of his chair, and there the two stood glaring upon each other, speechless. Each seemed to feel that this was no time for talking—that words were inadequate to do justice to the occasion. His Honor snatched up the docket with the evident intention of knocking Mr Thigpen down, whether in self-defence, or in vindication of the outraged dignity of the court, it was impossible to tell. Mr. Thigpen looked at it beseechingly—as much as to say, knock me down with it and welcome, but please don't hang me. There they stood for a quarter of a minute: then the judge, feeling doubtless that neither the penal code nor the court's discretion were adequate to punish the outrage as it deserved, said almost in a whisper, as the offender stood with his face untorted and unwiped:

'For God's sake be off from here, you cussed fool, and never let me see you again in this world.'

He made no unnecessary delay. When he had gotten fairly without hearing of the court, a crowd which had followed him were roaring around him with laughter.

'How did you feel, Allen?' asked one.

'Feel! I did'nt have no feelins. They was all scared out o' me.'

'But what did you carry him the money for?'

'Carry him the money? Wasn't that right? He found me.'

They whooped.

'I thought the money was his'n. I 'lowed that was the way he got his livin.'

'Gentlemen!' he resumed, when the crowd had recovered from the effect of this last remark, 'gentlemen, there's two things in this country that I'm agin. They are schools and court rooms. When I were standing thar jist now, if the feelins had not been skeered out o' me, and I had had my jedgment about me, I should a felt like little Asa Beatright used to feel when Iserl Meadows told him to go to horsin; and I had hoped never to have them feelins enduring my nat'ral life, because I had the conceptions from Asa's looks of what they must be. Gentlemen, I never seed a man before that I was afeerd of; I thought everybody was liable to come to court. Gentlemen, I comes no more without I'm fotcht. When I sneezed—and I couldn't ha' helped it, if the gallis had been right before me—when I sneezed, says I to myself, gone; when, ding my skin, ef I don't believe that's what scred me. Gentlemen I goes home;' and as they laughed and shouted, Mr. Thigpen left. Many and many times after that, even down to old age, he was heard to say that he had 'never seed but one man that he was afeerd of, and that was the jedge—old Jedge Mike, as used to be.'

CHAPTER V.

'Strain against Rickles!'

It was now Friday morning. The Judge was weary with the session, and fretful from repeated wranglings with several leading attorneys. These had all gone, the important cases having been tried or continued. The Court had announced its determination to adjourn that afternoon, whether the docket should be finished or not. It had not seen its family in two weeks, and it must and would see its family by to-morrow night. Juries and by-standers were quiet as mice. Mr. Sandidge was in the enjoyment of mild happiness, not only from the remembrance of having had a good run of luck during the week, but because the Judge was now in a hurry, and the case of Strain against Rickles was yet untried. He wished it continued, for he was of counsel for defendant, and their plea was doubtful.

'Strain vs. Rickles,' announced the Court, rapidly and fretfully, with pen in hand, as if to hint that it was expected to follow the fate of the half-dozen preceding cases, and be disposed of summarily.

'Ready for the plaintiff,' announced Mr. Mobley.

The Judge dropped his pen, leaned back in his chair, and cast a threatening look at the counsel. Mr. Sandidge merely remarked that that was a case in which some pints of law were involved, and as the Court was anxious to adjourn and to go home and see its family, he suggested that if the counsel was willing it might be continued generally. Mr. Mobley objecting to this disposition, he, after having a witness called, and receiving no answer, proceeded to make a showing for a continuance by the defendant. This was the absence of a witness who, as he had been informed, had said that he knew all about the case from beginning to end. It was in vain that Mr. Mobley urged the insufficiency of the showing for its indefiniteness, and the right of the opposing counsel to send for the witness who lived in the village, and who, as his client informed him, was then on the street and within hearing of the sheriff's call. He mentioned this fact and that his client had just passed him in the street, and heard him say when he was called. 'It is Sandidge. I know what he wants; he don't want me.'

'If the counsel or the court desires the presence of the witness, he can be procured in le s than five minutes by sending the sheriff for him. Do I un-

derstand that this court will continue a case and delay the rights of creditors
when it is assured that a witness who refuses to attend its summons is within
hearing of its officer's call—a witness whose acquaintance with the facts there
is only a hearsay and that the most indefinite—a witness who, to appearances,
is absent by the procurement, if not of the party at least of his counsel?'

The Judge hesitated. Mr. Sandidge seeing the effect upon both of them of
an exposure of, what was the fact, his instructions to the witness, not to obey
the call, withdrew his motion.

'I do this, may it please your Honor, not from anything my brother Mobley
has said in argument, or for his insinuations about procurements and such
like. The showing is a sufficient one ; but I'll waive it—I'll waive it, sir, and
I think I'm prepared—I say, I think I'm prepared (noticing the judge's dis-
satisfaction at the direction the matter was taking,) to end this matter very
summarily. The defendant is ready.'

A jury was impannelled, and Mr. Mobley proceeded with the case. It was
a simple action upon a promissory note given by defendant to plaintiff, who
was a merchant from Augusta. He read the declaration, exhibited the note
and closed.

Mr. Sandidge rose, and remarking that this was a case which he apprehended
would not long occupy the time of the court and the time of the county, announced to Mr. Mobley, that upon consulting his client, he had just ascertained that the consideration of the note sued on was usurious, and that his
conclusion being to rely on that defense solely, he should have to ask time of
the court in order to make out the plea, unless counsel would agree to consider
it in already.

Mr. Mobley, turning to his client, who assured him that it was not true,
allowed Mr. Sandidge to proceed.

A witness, the same who had been called, and whom Mr. Sandidge private-
ly sent for, went to the stand. After the usual preliminary that he did not
particularly charge his mind with what he heard and saw, not expecting to
be called on, he did remember that the parties said something about the note
being in renewal of accounts, some of which plaintiff himself had against defendant, and others of which he had traded to him; that he heard plaintiff tell
defendant that if he would give his note for them, adding in the interest, he
would indulge him a year on its payment ; that the defendant having agreed
to the proposition, gave his note, payable at twelve months. In answer to a
question from Mr. Mobley whether anything was said about extra interest, he
did not recollect as to that: didn't particularly charge his mind, not expecting to be called on. Mr. Sandidge offered in evidence the accounts with

legal interest computed in, acknowledging payment by note and bearing even
date with it. Then casting a triumphant smile at every body, he sat down.

Mr. Mobley looked at the judge with an expression which seemed to say :
'Surely, no fool, not even you, would admit such testimony.' The judge looked
at him, and his countenance seemed to ask, 'What do you say to that, Mr.
Mobley?' Mr. Mobley avowed his belief that in all judicial history, a thing
so absurd had never before been proposed, and he moved that the whole evidence be excluded, and he be allowed to take a verdict. Being called on for
his reasons : 'Because,' said he, contemptuously, 'it does not support the plea.
You have pleaded usury, and you have proved that the contract is not
usurious.'

Mr. Sandidge said that he might be mistaken ; that he said he might be
mistaken, but that he had never heard—he had now been practicing law
twenty-five years and better—but that to the best of his recollection, he had
never seen nor heard of a case where intere . was collected, or could be collected on open accounts, on accounts that were not liquidated.

'Who gainsays that ?' Mr. Mobley interposed.

'The counsel will please allow me to proceed, knowing as he does, his right
to reply. I said, may it please your Honor, that in my recollection, in a
practice now of twenty-five years and better, I had never seen nor heard of a
case where interest was collected or could be collected on open accounts—on
accounts that were not liquidated. That thing is for the first time in my
practice, sought to be enforced upon a court and upon a country. The plaintiff in this case—and these Augusty merchants——'

'Go on to the jury,' ordered the judge.

Mr. Sandidge bowed and turned to the jury.

'These Augus merchants, gentlemen of the jury,' 'easily resuming the
thread of his ar, .nent, 'these Augusty merchants, as a general thing, always
know what they are about. I say always—not a single exception ;' and he
bestowed on the plaintiff a look fully significant of his admission that he was
entitled to his si re of the encomium pronounced upon the class of which he
was an individual. 'These Augusty merchants know more in an hour than we
plain country peo le do in a week. And it is reasonable to suppose that they
do ; and 'tis because they are Angu ty merchants ; for what chauce have we
here in the country got to know as much as they know ? We don't see the
steam boats, and 'be power of the wagons, and th thousands of cotton bags
and the fine brick ware houses, and the hardware stores and the other stores that
always keep full of one particular kind of goods. If Tommy Rickles was to go to
Augusty, and was to want to buy a dog-knife for his little boy, he would just as apt

to go to a store which had nothing in it but calico and dry goods, and fuller of them than all the stores in this town ; and when they laughed and told him they were just out of that article, he might go to a hat store, and then into a shoe store, and then into a candy store—into a store where the shelves was literally blinded with jars of candy, and nothing but candy ; and so it might be an hour before he got to a hardware store and found a dog-knife for his little boy , and then ten to one, he couldn't find his way back to his wagon. I say we don't know any thing to compare with these Augusty merchants. But still there are some few things that we do know if we do live here in the country where there aint any steam boats, and hat stores, and candy stores, and hardware stores; and one of them is that you ce-ant collect interest on open accounts.'

That settled it Mr. Sandidge seemed to think ; and several of the jury, though evidently not yet very clear, inclined to think so too.

'We all know that,' continued Mr. Sandidge—'that is, all except Tommy Rickles.' (General lau- r, the jury seeing the matter a little more clearly especially as Tommy looked so innocent and pitiful.)

'And, gentlemen, Tommy knowed it too, if he had thought about it, and had'nt been with a Augusty merchant ; and bad'nt been thinking of the steamboats, and the power of the wagons, and the hat stores, and the shoe stores, and the hardware stores, and got his senses all confused up together.' (Continued laughter, a majority of the jury being fully satisfied.)

The judge waxing stern at the disorder, Mr. Sandidge had to moderate his humor, and concluded by arguing heatedly and seriously as he could, and even somewhat pathetically that interest not being collectible on open accounts, this plain principle vitiated the whole transaction and made it usurious. With another avowal of his desire not to take up the time of the court and the time of the country by arguing so plain a case, he sat down, his countenance expressing both a virtuous indignation at a great wrong which was attempted, and a proud satisfaction that it could not be done over his shoulders.

Mr. Mobley felt that, with the prejudices of the judge against himself and especially against usury, and the cunning Mr. Sandidge, he was in great danger of losing his case. He spoke with great energy on the absurdity of the defendant's plea. In the midst of his argument, Mr. Sandidge asked him for his authorities. This was done to embarrass him and throw him off his guard, as he would have had to admit that there was no authority in point ; but he had now gotten too high to be reached by Mr. Sandidge.

'I am asked,' he said, 'for the production of authority that the giving of a note in liquidation of a just debt is not usurious. I am asked for this by a lawyer of twenty-five years' practice—a lawyer who is old enough and prominent enough to be, what it especially behooves every lawyer to be, a conservator of public tranquility and private integrity—one who, with all his boasted contempt of legal precedents, and his real ignorance of them, yet knows full well that in no court of justice, even the most insignificant was this question, or any other one so absurd as this, ever raised; and whose only reason for raising it at this time, was his knowledge of the existence of dishonest habits and unreasonable prejudices which, as a leading citizen he ought to be one of the last to encourage. Violent as the presumption often is, and far from the very semblance of truth, it is, nevertheless, a presumption that judges know the laws; and it ought to be the habit of attorneys and solicitors, especially those of experience and influence, to refrain from raising questions, a moment's entertainment of which by any court is sufficient to deprive it of the respect of all men. But it has remained for this day to witness that the highest court in one of the sovereign States of this Confederacy, shall be insulted in its dignity and majesty by a course of conduct which seems to have been designedly pursued in order to test the sanity of that court's presiding officer. Assuredly to no other mind than to that of the counsel had it been possible to fail to occur, that an insignificant advantage in a suit at law was scarcely worth the having when it was to be gained in a way which, to say nothing of its influence upon its client, would establish either the stultification of the court, or (and he looked fixedly and fearlessly into the judge's face,) raise the suspicion of a yet greater infirmity. Even if he should consider himself as so great a friend to the court, whether from past favors or present adulation, or from any other cause, as to think himself entitled to the exalted privilege of being its favorite, one would have supposed that, if for no other reason, at least from motives of prudence and decency, he would have confined his conduct within that sphere where there would have been left at least a doubt as to what judgment that conduct ought to receive. It is a duty which we owe even to our private friends, not to demand a service of which there can be found no reason but friendship to justify the rendering, while every other reason but friendship would demand its refusal. There are some services which no ardor of friendship is adequate to procure—some indeed which a proper and worthy friendship would be the last to exact.'

A large crowd had gathered into the court room, attracted by the vehemence of the young lawyer's declamation. He was an eloquent speaker, and his speech was telling upon the bystanders. He saw it, and it stimulated him to continually increasing endeavor.

'There is a vulgar maxim that there is nothing to be lost by the asking of favors. The counsel has long and well learned how to profit by it. His suc-

ceseful experience in this respect, while it reflects no great honor upon his
sincerity or even upon his ingenuity, pays a consideration to the source from
which these favors flow, which it is impossible to be considered as in the smallest degree respectful. I warn him this day of the necessity to beware how he
abuses an influence which his every action shows that he is conscious of exerting.

There is a decorum which men, even of the greatest ability, when in the enjoyment of honors, even those the most fairly won, cannot neglect with impunity.
Let those, then, especially beware, the success of whose career is mainly depend-
ent upon favor. For granting that the power which, strange as it is, he may
truly think that he has immeasurably above others succeeded in conciliating,
and controlling, is absolute and unlimited, yet when it shall at last of all others
become convinced that such a control is no longer compatible, not only with the
appearance of respectability, but even with its own security, and shall, as it
assuredly will, withdraw from him the favor in which he seems to live, and move,
and have his being, he must then know how vain will be the late pursuit of
those other and higher means of success which it has been his constant habit to
neglect. And even if this should not come to pass, if dullness shall never be
ble to be conscious of, and to resist a control which binds it like the spell of
the charmer, surely, in a country so free and so usage in all its institutions
except its courts of justice, in a country where are so many good and
brave men—men who have been good enough and brave enough to resist and to
destroy every other form of tyranny, it is not too much to expect that the time
must come and come soon, when this last form must yield to the necessities of
an advanced civilization, and follow the fate of those which have gone before
it. Surely, it cannot long remain, that a free people, who have broken
the last shackle of political despotism, must continue to bow in abject submission before another which is the more odious, because their own hands have
created it, and because their own hands may peaceably destroy it.'

Mr. Mobley spoke for half an hour in this strain, during many parts of
which, Mr. Sandidge, smiling as he was, was rather piteous to be seen; and
when he spoke of the merits of the plea itself, Tommy Rickles but that he had
the great Mr. Sandidge for his friend, would have felt as if he ought to be in the
penitentiary.

The judge had once or twice opened his mouth for the purpose of arresting
the speaker and fining him for contempt; but Mobley's passion had terrified his
weak mind, and he had not the nerve to do it. When the last sentence of this
terrible philippic was spoken, with feeble desperation he beckoned the sheriff to
him. His adversary paused, and fixed his eyes, which rolled and burned like
the lion's, upon both of them alternately. The poor creature quailed, shrank

back in his chair, and bowed his head in the unutterable anguish of feeling that one more, and he a mere boy, had assaulted him in his very castle, and vanquished him. He dwelt in the latter part of his speech most solemnly upon the grave responsibilities of courts, which sat in the last resort upon the trial of the rights of citizens, In the absence of a high court for the correction of errors, every judge should, and every upright one would hesitate in pronouncing a judgment which was to be final and irrevocable. With some of the most eloquent and touching observations upon this sentiment, he closed his speech.

His Honor had determined to charge the jury in favor of the defendant. He was from principle and from habit (a habit much more common then than now) opposed to the payment of interest on open accounts ; and from principle and habit much more opposed to the payment of usurious interest. He had gotten it into his head that not only was usury condemned in the Bible, but that it had been mainly instrumental in the overthrow of the great empires of the ancient world, particularly the Roman. For some wag had told him that the latter was once publicly sold and bought by a celebrated usurer, one Didy Julian, under an execution of fieri facias. Being by his position, one of the conservators of the public safety, he had resolved to prevent if possible any such disaster to his native country, by rebuking and punishing this greatest vice of society whenever it came in his way, let it assume whatever disguise it might. In this renewal of open accounts, he imagined that he dimly perceived an attempt to evade the law, and had made up his mind when Mr. Sandidge had concluded, to charge upon it like a squadron of horse. But Mobley had, in the very absence of all opportunity of argument, cast such an amount of ridicule upon that motion, that he gravely doubted whether such a charge be right. Besides, Mobley had now risen to the rank of those whose ridicule and contempt he was ashamed and afraid to incur. He, therefore refused sullenly to give any instructions; but ordering the pleadings to be handed to the jury, sent them to their room. Half an hour afterwards having returned to the box, they were asked if they had agreed upon a verdict. The foreman, a little dark man, with short, straight up hair, and a sharp voice, rose and said :

'May it please the cote, we has not ; we desires to ask your Honor. if upon the provosa —'

'I don't want to hear of your provosocs. Go back to your room, and find a verdict, or make a mis-trial, I have no instructions to give on your provosoes.'

The little man dodged, turned quickly and led his followers back. They agreed to disagree ; ten of the number not being able to see any usury in the consideration, while two Sandidge men contended then, and ever afterwards persisted in contending, that it was plain as day.

And now it was the afternoon ; the sun was fast declining. Unless the court could get fifteen or twenty miles on its way home to-day, it would not reach it, and see its family by to-morrow night. Business had to be despatched right away everybody knew, or he left undone. Mr. Mobley had a money rule to take against the sheriff. That keeper of the county had been in some anxiety all the forenoon on account of it, but now he was at his ease since he had consulted Mr. Sandidge.

'What are you scared about ?   Don't you see that he's bent on starting home this evening ?'

'But I can't make a showing, because I've spent the money.'

'How much have you got about you at this particular time ?'

'Twenty dollars.'

'Hand it over to me.   It will do for you and me too for the present.'

The sheriff paid it over.

The last docket was closed ; in the intermission of court for dinner, the jury for the next term had been drawn ; those of this term were discharged. The judge took out his watch.

'May it please your Honor,' began Mr. Mobley, 'I desire to take a rule against the sheriff.'

'Will it be resisted ?'

'It will, may it please your Honor,' answered Mr. Sandidge. 'Mr. Sheriff go to my office and bring me the Acts of the last Legislature. Bring those of the two last, if you please, Mr. Sheriff. I disremember which it is that contains the law I wish to refer to. I ask the indulgence of the court for only a few minutes until I can make out the showing.

'Will there be any other rules or orders to be made ?' asked the judge impatiently.

'I have several,' Mr. Sandidge answered; 'but unless your Honor could hold over to-morrow, I shall be obliged to postpone taking them until the next term, as this rule will take up all the balance of this afternoon, probably.

The sheriff was going slowly towards the door ; 'come back here, sir,' bawled the judge, rising, his temper all gone. 'This court has got powers ; it may be insulted ; it may be abused ; but it has got powers ; it has got privileges ! Adjourn this court till the court in course !!'

'I protest against this disgraceful——,' began Mr. Mobley, but the sheriff in thundering tones was already announcing the adjournment, and as his Honor, pale and haggard rushed rapidly past him, 'God save the State,' he cried in thankful glee, 'and the onorble court !'

Mr. Mobley was too full of indignation to trust himself with many words.

'You two and he form a glorious trio in the dispensation of humane justice,' he said bitterly to the sheriff and his lawyer. 'But,' raising his hand and shaking it towards the latter, 'your day is passing ; mine is coming.'

'I think he will have to wait for his Supreme Court, eh, Mr. Sandidge?' remarked the sheriff as Mobley, taking the arm of Overton, who had staid till the last moment, walked away to his office.

Mr. Sandidge made no answer, but taking a big chew, smiled thoughtfully and seriously. In twenty minutes from that time, the two rascals compelled the plaintiff in execution, who had sought the rule, to settle his debt by taking the sheriff's note at twelve months without interest, also deducting the fee which had been paid to Mr. Sandidge for defending him as he said 'from them disgraceful proceedances.'

'And what do you think of Georgia justice?' asked Mr. Mobley, after he had reached his office.

'Our courts make as good a show as a caravan of wild beasts, do they not?'

'Such scenes as those to-day must surely happen very seldom.'

'Seldom ! I tell you they happen frequently.'

'In all the circuits?'

'No : in some of them, thank God, there are men who are neither fools nor rascals. But our miserable judiciary system will not allow a man to remain very long on the bench, however learned and upright he may go upon it, without his at least tending to become one or the other of these characters. The possession of unlimited power makes tyrants of the very best men, while it is notorious that our judges when they come off the bench are worse lawyers than they are when they go upon it. Why, what you saw is no worse than what has frequently occurred here. The miserable dolt used to crowd me, until I felt that I must resist or be a collared slave. He knows now, however, I think, that I am not afraid of him.'

'He is now evidently afraid of you.'

'I do not know as to that.' Mr. Mobley brushed the hair from his forehead, and looked as though he did know as to that.

'You have passed your ordeal at last, and will hereafter be able at least to divide the control of the court.'

'Do you think so ?'

'There is no doubt of it. He is evidently hacked.'

'I hope you are not mistaken ; for humiliating as it is to a gentleman's sense of propriety and decency, he must, in order to attain professional success, either become a favorite of the court or make the court afraid of him. Between the two, unhappy as is the choice of either, he cannot for a moment hesitate.'

The student made no answer, but parted with him, and having ordered his horse, rode slowly back to Mr. Parkinson's.

HOW MR. BILL WILLIAMS TOOK THE RESPONSIBILITY.

CHAPTER I.

"Our honor teacheth us
That we be bold in every enterprise."

The incidents that I am about to relate transpired near Dukes-borough, a small village something under a hundred miles from Augusta. For many years it has ceased even to be mentioned, except by the very few persons now living, who knew it before the Dukes, (from whom it was named,) left it. It has suffered the most absolute decay that I have ever known to befall a village. It had not been laid off in its beginning upon any definite plan. It seemed, indeed, to have become a village unexpectedly to itself and to everybody else, notwithstanding the fact that, instead of being in a hurry to become so, it took its own time, and that amounted to some years. The Dukes first established a blacksmith's shop—then a store. Both prospered. After some time other persons came in, and buying a little ground, settled on both sides of the road, (a winding road it was,) until there were several families, a school, and a church. Then the Dukes grew ambitious, and had the place called Dukes-borough. It grew on until this family left the place, some for the counties farther west, and some for the grave. Then decay set in at once, and to day a wretched log house on one side of the present road, and fit to be used for no purpose whatever, is the only sign of a relic of ancient Dukesborough.

It would be useless to speculate upon the causes of its fall. The places of human habitation are like those who inhabit them. Some persons die in infancy, some in childhood, some in youth, some at middle age, some at three score and ten, and some linger yet longer. But the last, in their own times, die as surely as many of the former. Methusaleh lived to nine hundred and sixty and eight years, but then he died. The account in Genesis, of those first generations of men, is, after all, I think, a melancholy one. The three last words, closing the history of every one of them, are to me very sad, 'And he died.'

So it is with the places wherein mortals dwell. Some of them become villages, some towns, some cities; but all—villages, towns, and cities, have their times to fall, just as infants, youths, men and old men, have theirs to die. People may say what they please about the situation not being well chosen, and about the disagreeableness of having the names of their residences all absorbed by the Dukes whom few persons used to like. This might be true, and I admit was true in this case. Yet, my position about Dukesborough is that it had lived out its life. It had run its race like all other things, places and people, who have lived out their lives and run their race; and when that was done, Dukesborough had to fall. It had not lived long, and it had run but slowly, if, indeed it can be said to have run at all. But it reached its journey's end. When it did, it had to fall; and it fell. It not often happens that I pass the place where it used to stand, but whenever I do, I feel somewhat as I feel when I go near the neglected grave of an old acquaintance. I say to myself in the latter case. Here is the last of him. He was once a stout, hearty, good-humored fellow. It is sad to think of him as having dropped everything, and being covered up here where the earth above him is now like the rest all around the place, and his grave, but for my recollection of the spot where it was dug, would be indistinguishable. But it could not be helped, and here he is for good. So of Dukesborough. When I pass along the road, I think, 'Here was once a smart village,'—no great things of ourse, but still a lively, busy, harmless village. It might have stood longer, and the rest of the world not have been hurt; but it is no use to think about it, because the thing is over, and Dukesborough is no more. Besides myself there may be one or two persons yet living, who can tell with some approximation to accuracy, where it used to stand. When we are dead, whoever may wish to gather any relic of Dukesborough, must do as they do on the supposed sites of the cities of more ancient times,—that is to say, they must dig for it.

These reflections, somewhat grave I admit, may seem to be unfitly preliminary to the narrative which is to follow them. But I trust they will be pardoned in an old man who could not forbear to make them, when calling to mind the forsaken places of his boyhood; albeit, the scenes which he proposes to describe, so far from being serious, are rather sportive in their character. If I can smile, and sometimes I do smile at the recital of things that were done and words that were said by some of my earliest cotemporaries, yet I must be allowed also a sigh when I remember that the doings and the sayings of nearly all of them are ended for this world.

CHAPTER II.

When Josiah Lorriby came into the neighborhood to keep a school, I was too young and too small to go to it alone. Having no older brother or sister to go along with me, my parents, although they were anxious for me to begin, were about to conclude to give it up, when, fortunately, it was ascertained that William Williams, a big fellow, whose widowed mother resided near to us, intended to go one term and complete his education, preparatory to being made the better fitted for a prospect of some ambition which he had in view. His way lay by our door, and as he was one of the most accommodating persons in the world, he kindly proffered to take charge of me. Without a moment's hesitation, and with much gratitude, this offer was accepted, and I was delivered over into his keeping.

William Williams was so near being a man that the little boys use to call him, Mr. Bill Williams, usually wore a stout dress-coat of homespun, with pockets opening upon the outer instead of the inner side of the skirts. Many a time, when I was fatigued with walking, have I ridden upon his back, my hands resting upon his shoulders and my feet standing in those capacious pockets. Mr. Bill promised to take care of me, and he kept his word.

On the first morning when the school was opened, we went together to it. About one mile and a half distant stood the school-house. Eighteen by twenty feet were its dimensions. It was built of logs and covered with clap-boards. It had one door, and opposite to that a hole in the wall, two feet square, which was called the window. It stood in the corner of a field (having formerly been used as a fodder-house,) and on the brow of a hill, at the foot of which, overshadowed by oak trees, was a noble spring of fresh water. Our way led us by this spring. Just as we reached it, Mr. Bill pointed to the summit and said :

'Yonder it is, Squire.'

Mr. Bill frequently called me squire, partly from mere facetious-ness, and partly from his respect for my father, who was a Justice of the Peace.

I did not answer. We ascended the hill, and Mr. Bill led me into the presence of the genius of the place.

Mr. Josiah Lorriby was a remarkable man, at least in appearance. He was below the middle height, but squarely built. His body was good enough, but his other parts were defective. He had a low flat head, with very short hair and very long ears. His arms were reasonably long, but his hands and legs were disproportionately short. Many tales were told of his feet, which he wore in shoes with iron soles. He was sitting on a split-bottom chair, on one side of the fire-place. Under him, with his head peering out between the rounds, sitting on his hind legs, and standing on his fore legs, was a small yellow dog, without tail or ears. This dog's name was Rum. How he came by it I never knew. It was, I suppose, given merely arbitrarily. I have frequently had occasion to notice that school-masters, as a class, are wont to bestow uncommon names upon not only their children, but their dogs, and even their horses, whenever they appear to have any of the last mentioned species of property.

On the other side of the fire-place, in another split bottom, sat a tall, raw-boned woman, with the reddest eyes that I have ever seen. This was Mrs. Mehitable, Mr. Lorriby's wife.

When I had surveyed these three personages,—this satyr of a man, this tailless dog, and this red-eyed woman, a sense of fear and helplessness came over me, such as I had never felt before, and have never felt since. I looked at Mr. Bill Williams, but he was observing another pupil and did not notice me. The other pupils, eighteen or twenty in number, seemed to be in deep meditation. My eyes passed from one to another of the objects of my dread, but they became finally fastened upon the dog. His eyes also had wandered, but only with vague curiosity around upon all the pupils, until they became finally fixed upon me. We gazed at each other several moments. Though he sat still, and I sat still, it seemed to me that we were drawing continually nearer to each other. Suddenly I lifted up my voice and screamed with all my might. It was so sudden and sharp that every body except the woman jumped. She indifferently pointed to the dog. Her husband arose, came to me, and in soothing tones asked what was the matter.

'I am scared!' I answered, as loud as I could speak.

'Scared of what, my little man? of the dog?'

'I am scared of all of you!'

He laughed with good humor, bade me not be afraid, called up Rum, talked to us both, enjoined upon us to be friends, and prophecied that we would be such—the best that had ever been in the world. The little creature became cordial at once, reared his fore feet upon his master, took them down, reared them upon me, and in the absence of a tail to wag, twisted his whole hinder parts in most violent assurance that if I should say the word we were friends already. Such kindness, and so unexpected, dissolved my apprehensions. I was in a condition to accept terms far less liberal. So I acceded, and went to laughing outright. Every body laughed, and Rum, who could do nothing better in that line, ran about and barked as joyously as any dog with a tail could have done. In the afternoon when school was dismissed, I invited Rum to go home with me; but he, waiting as I supposed, for a more intimate acquaintance, declined.

CHAPTER III.

It was delightful to consider how auspicious a beginning I had made. Other little boys profited by it. Mr. Lorriby had no desire to lose any of his scholars, and we all were disposed to make as much of advantage as possible of his apprehension, however unfounded, that on account of our excessive timidity, our parents might remove us from the school. Besides, we knew that we were to lose nothing by being on friendly terms with Rum. The dread of the teacher's wife soon passed away. She had but little to say and less to do. Nobody had any notion of any reason which she had for coming to the school. At first she occasionly heard a spelling class recite. After a little time she began to come much less often. and in a few weeks her visits had decreased to one in several days.

Mr. Lorriby was not of the sort of schoolmasters whom men use to denominate by the title of knock-down and drag out. He was not such a man as Israel Meadows. But although he was good hearted enough, he was somewhat politic also. Being a new comer, and being poor, he determined to manage his business with due regard to the tastes, the wishes, and the prejudices of the community in which he labored. He decidedly preferred a mild reign but it was said he could easily accommodate himself to those who required a more vigorous policy. He soon learned that the latter was the favorite here. People complained that there was little or no whipping. Some who had read the fable of the frogs who desired a sovereign, were heard to declare that Josiah Lorriby was no better than 'Old King-Log.' One patron spoke of taking his children home, placing the boy at the plough and the girl at the spinning wheel.

Persons in those days loved their children, doubtless, as well as now; but they had some strange ways of showing their love. The strangest of all was the evident gratification which the former felt when the latter were whipped at school. While they all had a notion that education was something which it was desirable to get, it was believed that the impartation of it needed to be conducted in most mysterious ways. The school-house of that day was, in a manner, a cave of Trophonius, into which urchins of both sexes entered amid certain incomprehensible ceremonies, and were everlastingly subject and used to be whirled about. body and soul, in a vortex of confusion. I might pursue the analogy and say that, like the votaries of Trophonius, they were not wont to smile until long after this violent and rotary indoctrination, but rather to weep and lament, unless they were brave like Apollonius, or big like Allen Thigpen, and so could bully the priest far enough to have the bodily rotation dispensed with. According to these notions, the principles of the education of books were not to be addressed to the mind and to the heart; but, if they were expected to stick, they must be beaten with rods into the back. Through this ordeal of painful ceremonies had the risen generation gone, and through the same ordeal they honesty believed that the present generation ought to go, and must go. No exception was made in favor of genius. Its back was to be kept as sore as stupidity's; for, being yoked with the latter, it must take the blows, the oaths, and the imprecations. I can account for these things in no other way than by supposing that the o'd set of persons I ad come out of the old system, with minds so bewildered as to be ever afterwards incapable of thinking upon it in a reasonable manner. In one respect there is a considerable likeness between mankind and some individuals of the brute creation. The dog seems to love best that master who beats him before giving him a bone. I have heard persons say, (those who had carefully studied the nature and habits of the mule,) that he is wont to evince a gratitude, somewhat touching, when a bundle of fodder is thrown to him, at the close of a day on which he has been driven within an inch of his life. So with the good people of former times. They had been beaten so constantly, and so mysteriously at school, that they seemed to entertain a grateful affection for it ever afterwards. It was, therefore, with feelings of benign satisfaction, sometimes not unmixed with an innocent gayety of mind, that they were wont to listen to their children when they complained of the thrashings they daily received some of which would be wholly unaccountable. Indeed the latter sort seemed to be considered, of all others, the most salutary. When the punishment was graduated by the offense, it was supporting too great a likeness to the affairs of every day life and, therefore, wanting in solemn impressiveness. But when a school master, for no accountable reason, whipped a boy, and so set his mind in a state of utter bewilderment as to what could be the matter, and the most vague speculations upon what was to become of him in this world, to say nothing of the next, ah! then it was that the experienced felt a happiness that was gently exstatic. They recurred in their minds to their own school time, and they concluded that, as these things had not killed them, they must have done them good. So some of our good mothers in Israel, on occasions of great religous excitement, as they bend over a shrieking sinner, smile in serene happiness as they fan his throbbing temples, and fondly encourage him to shriek on; thinking of the pit from which they were digged, and of the rock upon which now they are standing, they shout, and sing, and fan, and fanning ever, continue to sing and shout.

CHAPTER IV

When Mr. Lorriby had jerked the depth of public affection, he became a new man. One Monday morning be announced to all going to turn over a new leaf, and he went straightway to turning it. Before night several boys, from small to medium, had been flogged. He had not begun on the girls except in one instance. In that I will remember the surprize I felt at the manner in which her case was disposed of. Her name was Susan Potter. She was about twelve years old, and well grown. When she was called up, inquiry was made by the master if any boy present was willing to take upon himself the punishment which must otherwise fall upon her. After a moment's silence, Seaborn Byne, a boy of fourteen, rose and presented himself. He was good tempered and fat, and his pants and round jacket fitted him closely. He advanced with the air of a man who was going to do what was right, with no thought of consequences. Miss Potter unconcernedly went to her seat.

But Seaborn soon evinced that he was dissatisfied with a bargain that was so wholly without consideration. I believed then, and I believe to this day but for his being so good a mark he would have received fewer stripes. But his round fat body and legs stood so temptingly before the rod, and the latter fell upon good flesh so entirely through its whole length, that it was really hard to stop. He roared with pain so unexpectedly severe, and violently rubbed each spot of recent infliction. When it was over he came to his seat and looked at Susan Potter. She seemed to feel like laughing. Seaborn got no sympathy, except from a source, which he despised, that was his younger brother, Joel. Joel was weeping in secret.

'Shut up your mouth,' whispered Seaborn, threateningly—and Joel shut up.
Then I distinctly heard Seaborn mutter the following words:
'Ef I ever takes another for her, or for any of 'em, may I be dinged, and then dug up and dinged over again.'

I have no doubt that he kept his oath, for I continued to know Seaborn Byne until he was an old man, and I never knew a person who persistently held that vicarious system of school punishment in deeper disgust. What his ideas were about being 'dinged,' and about that operation being repeated, I did not know, but I supposed that was something, that, if possible, better be avoided.

Such doings as these made a great change in the feelings of us little ones. Yet I continued to run the crying schedule. It failed at last, and I went under.

Mr. Lorriby laid it upon me remorselessly. I had never dreamed that he would give me such a flogging—me who considered myself, as every body else considered me—a favorite. Now the charm was gone ; the charm of security. It made me very sad. I lost my love for the teacher. I even grew cold towards Rum, and Rum in his turn grew cold towards me.

In a short time Mr. Lorriby had gone as nearly all around the school as it was prudent to go. Every boy but two had received his portion,—some once, some several times. These two were Mr. Bill Williams, and another big boy, named Jeremiah Hobbes. These were, of course, as secure against harm from Mr. Lorriby as they would have been had he been in Guinea. Every girl also had been flogged, or had had a boy flogged for her, except Betsy Ann Acry. the belle of the school. She was a light-haired, blue-eyed, plump, delicious looking girl, fourteen years old. Now for Miss Betsy Ann Acry, as it was known to every body about the school house, Mr. Bill Williams had a partiality which, though not avowed, was decided. He had never courted her in set words, but he had observed her from day to day, and noticed her ripening into womanhood, with constantly increasing desire. He was scarcely a match for her even if they both had been in condition to marry. He knew this very well. But considerations of this sort seldom do a young man any good. More often

than otherwise they make him worse. At least such was their effect upon Mr.
Bill. The greater the distance ' etween dim and Miss Betsy Ann, the more he
yearned across it. He sat in school where he could always see her, and oh !
how he eyed her. Often, often have I noticed Mr. Bill, leaning the side of his
head upon his arms, extended on the desk in front of him, and looking at her
with a countenance which, it seemed to me, ought to have made some impression. Betsy Ann received all of this as if it was no more than she was entitled to, but showed no sign whether she set any value upon the possession or
not. Mr. Bill hoped she did ; the rest of us believed she did not.

Mr. Bill had another ambition, which was, if possible, even higher than the
winning of Miss Acry. Having almost extravagant notions of the greatness
of Dukesborough, and the distinction of being a resident within it, he had long
desired to go there as a clerk in a store. He had made repeated applications
to be taken in by Messrs. Bland & Jones, and it was in obedience to a hint from
those gentlemen that he had determined to take a term of finishing off at the
school of Mr. Lorriby. This project was run out of his mind, even in moments
of his fondest imaginings about Miss Betsy Ann. It would have been not easy
to say which he loved the best. The clerkship seemed to become nearer and
nearer, after each Saturday's visit to town, until at last he had a distinct offer
of the place. The salary was small, but he waived that consideration in view of
the exaltation of the office, and the greatness of living in Dukesborough. He
accepted, to enter upon his duties in four weeks, when the quarter session of the
school would expire.

The dignified ways of Mr. Bill after this, made considerable impression upon
all the school. Even Betsy Ann condescended to turn her eyes oftener in the
direction where he happened to be, and he was almost inclined to glory in the
hope that the possession of one dear object would draw the other along with it.
At least he felt that if he should lose the latter, the former would be the
highest consolation which he could ask. The news of the distinguished honor
that had been conferred upon him, reached the heads of the school early on the
Monday following the eventful Saturday when the business was done. I say
heads, for of late Mrs. Mehitable came with her husband almost every day.
She received the announcement without emotion. Mr. Lorriby, on the other
hand, in spite of the prospect of losing a scholar, was almost extravagant in his
congratulations.

'It was a honor to the whole school,' he said.

'I feels it myself. Sich it war under all the circumstances. It was obleeged
to be, and sich it war, and as it war sich, I feels it myself.'

Seaborn Byne heard this speech. Immediately afterwards he turned to me
and whispered the following comment :

'He be dinged ! The deceatful old son-of-a-bitch !'

CHAPTER V.

It was the unanimous opinion amongst Mr. Lorriby's pupils that he was
grossly inconsistent with himself ; that he ought to have begun with the rigid
policy at first, or to have held to the mild. Having once enjoyed the sweets
of the latter, thoughts would occasionally rise and questions would be asked.
Seaborn Byne was not exactly the head, but he was certainly the orator of a
revolutionary party. Not on his own account, for he had never yet, except as
the voluntary substitute of Miss Susan Potter, felt upon his own body the

effects of the change of discipline. Nor did he seem to have any apprehension on that score. He even went so far as to say to Mr. Bill Williams, who had playfully suggested the bare idea of such a thing, that 'ef o'd Jo Lorriby raised his o'd pole on him, he wou d put his lizzard,' (as Seaborn facetiously called his knife) 'into his paunch. This threat had made his brother Joel extremely unhappy. His little heart was bowed down with the never resting fear and belief that Seaborn was destined to commit the crime of murder upon the body of Mr. Lorriby. On the other hand Seaborn was constantly vexed by the sight of the course of floggings which Joel received. Poor Joel had, somehow, in the beginning of his studies, gotten upon the wrong road, and as nobody ever brought .. . back to the starting point, he was destined, it seemed, to wander about lost evermore. The more floggings he got, the more hopeless and wild were his efforts at extrication. It was unfortunate for him that his brother took any interest in his condition. Seaborn had great contempt for him, but yet he remembered that he was his brother, and his brother's heart wou'd not allow itself to feel no concern. That concern manifested itself in endeavoring to teach Joel himself out of school, and in flogging him himself, by way of preventing Joel' having to submit to that disgrace at the hands of old Joe. So eager was Seaborn in this brotherly design, and so indocile was Joel, that for every flogging which the latter received from the master, he got from two to three from Seaborn. Amongst all these evils, floggings from Mr. Lorriby, floggings from Seaborn, and the abiding apprehension that the former was destined to be killed by the latter, Joel Byne was a case which was to be pitied.

'It ar' a disgrace,' said Mr. Bill to me, one morning as we were going to school; 'and I wish Mr. Larrabee knowed it. Betwixt him and Sebe that little innercent individiel ar' bent eu bein' useded up. It beats all natur. Ole Larrabee ar' bad enough, but Sebe ar' wusser yit. The case ar' wusser than if there was two Larrabees'. In all my experence I has not seed jist sich a case. It ar' beyant hope.'

Mr. Bill's sympathy made him serious, and almost gloomy. I believe that at that moment both Betsy Ann Acry and the clerkship were out of his mind. The road on which the B....'s came to school met ours a few rods from the Spring, we were now at the ... er place. Mr. Bill had scarcely finished his last sentence when we h... d behind us the screams of a child. We should have been much alarmed if we had not known where they were and what was their cause.

'Thar it is agi ,' said Mr. Bill; 'at it good and soon. It do beat everything in this blessed world, ef it don't, ding me.'

We looked behind us. Here came Joel at full speed, hatless, his spelling book in one hand, and his dinner basket, without cover, hanging from the other, screaming wi h all his might. Fifty yards behind him ran Seaborn, who had been delayed, as it seemed, by having to stop to pick up the bucket cover and Joel's hat, as he had them both in his hands.

'Stop, you son ol-a-bitch,' he cried.

Just before reaching the spot where we were, he overtook the fugitive, threw him down, took out of his hand the spelling book, opened it, and then getting upon him, fastening his arms with his own knees, 'Now,' said he. 'you rascal, spell crucifix.'

Joel attempted to obey.

'S again, you little devil! S-i, s-i! Ding my skin, if you shan't larn it ef I have to cram every bit of it intoo your mouth with my fist.'

'Look a here, Sebe!' interposed Mr. Bill; 'fun's fun, but too much is too much.'

Now what these words were intended to be preliminary to, there was no opportunity of ascertaining; for just then Mr. Josiah Lorriby, who had diverged from his own way in order to drink at the spring, presented himself.

'What air you abont thar, Sebion Byne?'

Seaborn arose, and though he considered his conduct not only justifiable, but proper, he looked a little crest-fallen.

'Ah, indeed!' You're the assistant teacher, air you? Interfering with my business, and my rights, and my duties, and my —, here. Let us all go to the school-house now. Mr. Byne will manage business hereafter. I, as or me, I aint no whar now. Come, Mr. Byne, less go to school.'

Mr. Lorriby and Seaborn went on, side by side. Mr. Bill looked as if he were highly gratified. 'Ef he don't get it now, he never will.'

Alas for Joel! Delivered from Seaborn, he was yet more miserable than before, and he forgot his own griefs in his pity for the impending fate of Mr. Lorriby and his apprehension for the ultimate consequence of this day's work to his brother. He pulled me a little behind Mr. Bill, and tremblingly whispered:

'Poor Mr. Lorriby! Do you reckon they will hang Seaby, Phil?'

'What for!' I asked.

'For killing Mr Lorriby!'

I answered that I hoped not. This was as far as I could go, for I had some confidence myself in Seaborn's desperate resolution.

The matter was settled before we two had reached the house. As we got to the door Mr. Lorriby began to lay on, and Seaborn to roar. The laying on and the roaring lasted until the master was satisfied. Joel and I had staid outside. When it was over I looked into Joel's face. It was radiant with joyful smiles. Happy little fellow! Seaborn would not be hung! That delusion was gone forever.

CHAPTER VI.

Having broken the ice upon Seaborn, Mr. Lorriby went into the sport of flogging him whenever he felt like it. Seaborn's revolutionary sentiments grew deeper and stronger constantly. But he was now, of course, hopeless of accomplishing any results himself, and he knew that the only chances were to enlist Jeremiah Hobbs, or Mr. Bill Williams, and make him the leader in the enterprise. Very soon, however, one of these chances was lost. Hobbes received and accepted an offer to become an overseer, and Seaborn's hopes were now fixed upon Mr. Bill alone. That also was destined soon to be lost by the latter's prospective clerkship. Besides, Mr. Bill being even tempered, and never having received, and being never likely to receive any provocation from Mr. Lorriby, the prospect of making anything out of him was gloomy enough. In vain Seaborn raised innuendoes concerning his pluck. In vain he tried every other expedient, even to secretly drawing on Mr. Bill's slate a picture of a very little man flogging a very big boy, having written as well as he could, the name of Mr. Lorriby near the former, and that of Mr. Bill near the latter. Seaborn could not disguise himself, and Mr. Bill, when he saw the pictures, informed the artist that if he did not mind what he was about, he would get a worse beating than ever Joe Larrabee gave him. Seaborn had but one hope left; but that involved some little delicacy, and could be managed only by its own circumstances. It might do, and it might not do. If Seaborn had been a praying boy, he would have prayed that if anything was to be made out of this, it would come before Mr. Bill should leave. Sure enough it did come. Just one week before the quarter was out, it came. Seaborn was in ecstacies. Let us see what it was that so exalted him.

Miss Betsy Ann Acry had heretofore escaped correction for any of her short comings, although they were not few. She was fond of mischief, and no more afraid of Mr. Lorriby than Mr. Bill Williams was. Indeed, Miss Betsy Ann considered herself to be a woman, and she had been heard to say that a whipping was something which she would take from nobody. Mr. Lorriby smiled at her mischievous tricks, but Mrs. Lorriby frowned. These ladies became to dislike each other. The younger, when in her frolics, frequently noticed the elder give her husband a look which was expressive of much meaning. Seaborn had also noticed this, and the worse Miss Acry grew, the oftener Mrs. Lorriby came to the school. He had come to believe fully that the object which the female Lorriby had in coming at all was to protect the male. A bright thought! He communicated it to Miss Acry, and slyly hinted several times that he believed she was afraid of Old Red Eye, as he denominated the master's wife. Miss Acry indignantly repelled every such insinuation, and became only the bolder in what she said and what she did. Seaborn knew that the Lorriby's were well aware of Mr. Bill's preference for the girl, and he intensely enjoyed her temerity. But it was hard to satisfy him that she was not afraid of Old Red Eye. If Old Red Eye had not been there, Betsy Ann would have done so and so. The reason why she did not do so and so, was because old Red Eye was about. Alas for human nature—male and female! Betsy Ann went on and on, until she was brought to a halt. The occasion was thus:

There was in the school a boy, of about my own size, and of a year or two older, whose name was Martin Granger. He was somewhat of a pitiful looking creature—whined when he spoke, and was frequently in quarrels, not only with the boys, but with the girls. He was suspected of sometimes playing the part of spy and informant to the Lorriby's, both of whom treated him with more consideration than any other pupil received, except Mr. Bill Williams. Miss Betsy Ann cordially disliked him, and she honored myself by calling me her favorite in the whole school.

Now Martin and myself got ourselves very unexpectedly into a fight. I had divided my molasses with him at dinner time for weeks and weeks. A few of the pupils, whose parents could afford to have that luxury, were accustomed to carry it to school in vials. I usually ate my part, after boring a hole in my biscuit, and then filling it up. I have often wished, since I have been grown, that I could relish that preparation as I relished it when a boy. But as we grow older our tastes change. Martin Granger relished the juice even more than I. In all my observations, I have never known a person, of any description, who was as fond of molasses as he was. It did me good to see him eat it. He never brought any himself, but he used to hint, in his whining way, that the time was not distant when his father would have a whole keg full, and when he should bring it to school in his father's big snuff bottle, which was well known to us all. Although I was not so sanguine of the realization of this prospect as he seemed to be, yet I had not on that account became tired of furnishing him. I only grew tired of his presence while at my dinner, and I availed myself of a trifling dispute one day to shut down upon him. I not only did not invite him to partake of my molasses, but I rejected his proposition to do so without invitation. He had been dividing it with me so long that I believe he thought my right to cut him off now was stopped.' He watched me as I bored my holes, and poured in, and ate, and even wasted the precious fluid. I could not consume it all. When I had finished eating, I poured water into the vial; made what we called 'beverage.' I would drink a little, then shake it and hold it up before me. The golden bubbles shown gloriously in the sun light. I had not said a word to Martin during these interesting operations, nor even looked towards him. But I knew that his eyes were upon me and the vial. Just as I swollowed the last drop, his full heart could bear no more, and he uttered a cry of pain. I turned to him and asked him what was the matter. The question seemed to be considered as adding insult to injustice.

'Corn deternally trive your devilish hide,' he answered, and gave me the full benefit of his clenched hand upon my stomach. He was afterwards heard to say that 'thar was the place whar he wanted to hit fust.' We closed, scratched, pulled hair, and otherwise struggled until we were separated. Martin went immediately to Mr. Lorriby, gave his version of the brawl, and just as the school was to be dismissed for the day, I was called up and flogged without inquiry and without explanation.

Miss Betsy Ann Acry had seen the fight. When I came to my seat, crying bitterly, her indignation could not contain itself.

'Mr. Lorribee,' she said, her red checks growing redder, 'you have whipped that boy for-nothing.'

Betsy Ann, with all of her pluck, had never gone so far as this. Mr. Lorriby turned pale and looked at his wife. Her red eyes fairly glistened with fire. He understood it, and said to Betsy Ann in a hesitating tone,—

'You had better keep your advice to yourself.'

'I did not give you any advice. I just said you whipped that boy for nothing, and I said the truth.'

'Aint that advice, madam?'

'I am no madam, I thank you, sir ; and if that's advice —'

'Shet up your mouth, Betsy Ann Acry.'

·Yes sir,' said B. A., very loud, and she fastened her pretty, pouting lips to gether, elevated her head, inclined a little to one side, and seemed amusedly awaiting further orders.

The female Lorriby here rose, went to her husband, and whispered earnestly to him. He hesitated and then resolved.

'Come here to me, Betsy Ann Acry.'

She went up as gaily as if she expected a present.

'I am going to whip Betsy Ann Acry. Ef any boy here wants to take it for her, he can now step forrards.'

Betsy Ann patted her foot, and looked neither to the right nor to the left, nor yet behind her.

When a substitute was invited to appear, the house was as still as a grave yard. I rubbed my legs apologetically, and looked up at Seaborn who sat by me.

'No sir ; if I do may I be dinged, and then dug up and —' I did not listen to the remainder, and as no one else seemed disposed to volunteer, and as the difficulty was brought about upon my own account, and as Betsy Ann liked me and I liked Betsy Ann, I made a desperate resolution, and rose and presented myself. Betsy Ann appeared to be disgusted.

'I don't think I would whip that child any more to-day if I wa in your place especially for other folk',doines.'

'That's jist as you say.'

'Well, I say go back to your seat, Phil.'

I obeyed, and felt relieved and proud of myself. Mr. Lorriby began to straighten his switch. Then I, and all the other pupils, looked at Mr. Bill Williams.

CHAPTER VII.

Oh! what an argument on was going on in Mr. Bill's breast. Vain had been all efforts. He had not been able to bring him in any way in collision with the Lorribies. He had even kept himself out of all combinations to get a little holiday by an innocent decsion. He needless had been all appeals, heretofore, to his sympathies; for he was the rest who had been through the ordeal of the school, and I led green to believe that it did more harm than good. If it had been any body but Betsy Ann Acry, he would have been unmoved. But it was Betsy Ann Acry, and he had been often heard to say that if Betsy Ann Acry should have to be whipped, he should take upon himself the responsibility of seeing that that must not be done. And now that contingency had come. What ought to be done? How was this responsibility to be discharged? Mr. Bill wished that the female Lorriby had stayed away that day. He did not know exactly why he wished it, but he wished it. To add to his other difficulties, Miss Betsy Ann had never given any token of her reciprocation of his regard; for now that the novelty of the future clerkship had worn away, she had returned to her old habit of never seeming to notice that there was such a person as himself. But the idea of a switch falling upon her, whose body, from the crown of her head to the soles of her feet, was so precious to him, outweighed every other consideration, and he made up his mind to be as good as his word, and *take the responsibility*. Just as the male Lorriby, (the female by his side,) was about to raise the switch.

'Stop a minute, Mr. Lorrabee,' he exclaimed, advancing in a highly excited manner.

The teacher lowered his arm and retreated one step, looking a little irresolute. His wife advanced one step, and looking straight at Mr. Bill, her robust frame rose at least an inch higher.

'Mr. Larrabee! I— ah— don't exactly consider myself — ah— as a scholar here now; because— ah— I expect to move to Dukesborough in a few days, and keep store thar, for Mr. Bland and Jones.'

To his astonishment, this announcement, so impressive heretofore, failed of the slightest effect now, when, of all times, an effect was desired. Mr. Lorr'by, in answer to a sign from his wife, had recovered his lost ground, and looked placidly upon him, but answered nothing.

'I say,' repeated Mr. Bill distinctly, as if he supposed he had not been heard. 'I say that I expect in a few days to move to Dukesborough; to live thar, to keep store thar for Mr. Bland and Jones.'

'Well Williams, I think I have heard that before. I want to hear you talk about it some time when it aint school time, and when we aint so busy as we air now at the present.

'Well, but —' persisted Mr. Bill.

'Well, but?' enquired Mr. L.

'Yes sir,' answered the former, insistingly:

'Well but what? Is this case got anything to do with it? Is she got any thing to do with it?'

'In cose it have not,' answered Mr: B., sadly:

'Well, what makes you tell us of it now, at the present?' Oh! what a big word was that us, then, to Josiah Lorriby.

'Mr. Larrabee,' urged Mr. B., in as persuasive accents as he could employ; 'No sir, Mr. Larrabee, it have not got any thing to do with it; but yet —'

'Well—yit what, William?'

'Well, Mr. Lorrabee, I thought, as I was a goin to quit school soon; and as I was a goin to move to Dukesborough,—as I was a goin *right outin* your school, intoo Dukesborough as it war—to keep store thar—may be you mout, as a favor, do me a favor before I left.'

'Well! may I be dinged, and then dug up and dinged over agin!' This was said in a suppressed whisper, by a person at my side. 'Beggin! beggin! ding his white-livered hide—b-e-g-gin!'

'Why, William,' replied Mr. L.,' ef it ware convenant, and the favor war not too much, it mout be that I mout grant it.'

'I thought you would, Mr. Larrabee. The favor aint a big one. Least ways, it aint a big one to you. It would be a mighty —' But Mr. Bil thought he could hardly trust himself to say how big a one it would be to himself.

'Well, what is it, William?'

'Mr. Larrabee!— Sir, Mr. Larrabee, I ax 't as a faver of you, not to whip Betsy Ann—which is Miss Betsy Ann Acry.'

'Thar, now!' groaned Seabort.... and bowed his head in despair.

The male Larriby looked upon the female. Her face had relaxed somewhat from its stern expression. She answered his glance by one which implied a conditional affirmative.

'Ef Betsy Ann will behave herself, and keep her impudence to herself. I will let her off this time.'

All eyes turned to Betsy Ar.... I never saw her look so fine as she raised up her head, tossed her yellow ringlets back, and said, in a tone increasing in loudness from beginning to end:

'But Betsy Ann Acry wont do it.'

'Hello agin thar!' whispered Seaborn, and raised his head. His dying hopes of a big row were revived. This was the last opportunity, and he was as eager as if the last dollar he ever expected to make had been pledged upon the event. I have never forgotten his appearance, as with his legs wide apart, his hands upon his knees, his lips apart, but his teeth nearly closed, he gazed upon that scene.'

'Lorriby, the male, was considerably disconcerted, and would have compromised; but Lorriby, the female, again, in an instant, resumed her hostile attitude, and this time her great eyes looked like two balls of fire. She concentrated their gaze upon Betsy Ann, with a ferocity which was appalling. Betsy Ann tried to meet them, and did for one moment; but in another she found she could not hold out longer; so she buried her face in her hands and sobbed. Mr. Bill could endure no more.

'The fact ar',' he cried, 'that I am goin to *take* the respensibility. Consequences may be consequences, but I shall take the respensibility.' His countenance was that of a man who had made up his mind. It had come at last, and we were perfectly happy.

The female Lorraby turned her eye from Betsy Ann and fixed them steadily on Mr. Bill. She advanced a step forward, and raised her arms and placed them on her sides. The male Lorraby placed himself immediately behind his mate's right arm, while Rum, who seemed to understand what was going on, came up, and standing on his mistress's left, looked curiously up at Mr. Bill

Seaborn Byne noticed this last movement. 'Well, ef that don't beat crea tion. You in it, too, is you?' he muttered through his teeth. 'Well, never do you mind. Ef I don't fix you, and put you whar you'll never know no more but what you've got a tail, may I be dinged, and then, & c.

It is true that Seaborn had been counted upon for a more important work than the neutralizing of Rum's forces; still, I knew that Mr. Bill wanted and needed no assistance. We were all ready, however; that is, I should say all but Martin. He had no griefs, and therefore no desires.

Such was the height of Mr. Bill's excitement, that' he did not even seem to notice the hostile demonstrations of these numerous and various foes. His mind was made up, and he was going right on to his purpose.

'Mr. Lorrabee,' he said, firmly, 'I am goin to take the responsibility. I axed you as a favor to do me a favor before I left. I aint much used to axin favors; but sich it war now. It seems as ef that favor cannot be granted. Yea, sich is the circumstances. But it must be so. Sense I have been here they aint been no difficulties betwixt you and me, nor betwixt me and Miss Larrabee, and no nothin' of the sort, not even betwixt me and Rum. Sich, therefore, it was why I axed the favor us a favor. But it can't be hoped, and so I takes the responsi ability. Mr. Larrabee, sir, and you, Miss Larrabee, I am goin' from this school right intoo Dukesborough straight intoo Mr. Bland's store, to clerk thar. Sich bein' all the circumstances, I hates to do what I tell you I'm goin' to do. But it can't be hoped it seem, and I ar' goin' to do it

Mr. Bill announced this conclusion in a very ˻ elevated tone.
'Oh, yes, ding your old hides of you,' I heard ˻ do.

Mr. Larrabee, and you, Miss Larrabee,' cont˻ the speaker, 'I does not de ires that Betsy Ann Acry shall be whipped. ˻ on to say, that as sich it ar', and as sich the circumstances, Betsy Ann A˻ an't be whipped whar I ar' ef I can keep it from bein' done.'

'You heered that, didn't you?' asked Seaborn, low but cruelly triumphant; and Seaborn looked at Rum as if considering how he should begin the battle with him.

Mrs. Lorraby, seldom spoke. Whenever she did, it was to the point.
'Yes, but Weelliam Weelliams, you can't keep it from boin' done.' And she straightened herself yet higher, and raising her hands yet higher upon her sides, changed the angle of her elbows from obtuse to acute.
'Yes, but I kin,' persisted Mr. Bill. 'Mr. Larrabee! Mr. Larrabee!'

This gentleman had lowered his head, and was peering at Mr. Bill through the triangular opening formed by his taste's side and arm. The reason why Mr. Bill addressed him twice, was because he had missed him when he threw the first address over her shoulder. The last was sent through the triangle.

'Mr. Larrabee! I say it kin be done and I'm goin' to do it. Sir, little as I counted on sich a case, yit still, it ar' so. Let the consequences be what they be, both now and some futur day. Mr. Larrabee, sir, that whippin' that you was a goin' to give to Betsy Ann Acry cannot fall upon her shoulders, and— that is, upon her shoulders, and before my face. Instid of sich, sir, you may jist—iustid of whippin' her, ir, you may - instid of her give it sir — notwith standin' and nevertheless—you may give it to ME.'

CHAPTER VIII.

"Oh! what a fall was there, my countrymen!
Then you and I and all of us fell down!"

If the pupils of Josiah Lorriby's school had had the knowledge of all tongues; if they had been familiar with the histories of all the base men of all the ages, they could have found no words in which to characterize, and no person with whom to compare Mr. Bill Williams. If they had known what it was to be a traitor, they might have admitted that he was more alike this, the most despicable of all characters, than any other. But they would have argued that he was baser than all other traitors, because he had betrayed, not only others, but himself. Mr. Bill Williams, the big boy; the future resident of Dukesborough; the expectant clerk; the vindicator of persecuted girlhood, in the person of the girl he loved; the pledge-taker of responsibilities,—that he should have taken the pains, just before he was going away, to degrade himself by proposing to take upon his own shoulders the rod that had never before descended but upon the backs and legs of children! Poor Seaborn Byne! If I ever saw expressed in one human being's countenance, disgust, anger and abject hopelessness, I saw them as I turned to look at him. He spoke not one word, not even in whispers, but he looked as if he could never more place confidence in mortal flesh.

When Mr. Bill had concluded his ultimatum, the female Lorriby's arms came down, and the male Lorriby's head went up. They sent each the other a smile. Both were smart enough to be satisfied. The latter was more than satisfied.

"I am proud this day of William Williams. It air so, and I can but say I air proud of him. William Williams were now in a position to stand up and shine in his new spere of action. If he went to Dukesborough to keep store thar, he mout now go sayin' that as he had been a good scholar, so he mout expect to be a good clerk, and fit to be trusted, yea, with thousands upon thousands, ef sich mout be the case. But as it was so, and as he have been to us all as it ware, and no difficulties, and no nothin' of the sort, and he ware goin', and it mout be soon; yea, it mout be to-morrow, from this school straight intoo a store, I cannot, nor I cannot. No, far be it. This were a skene too solemn and too lovely for sich. I cannot, nor I cannot. William Williams may now take his seat.

Mr. Bill obeyed. I was glad that he did not look at Betsy Ann as she turned to go to hers. But she looked at him. I saw her, and little as I was, I saw also that if he ever had had any chance of winning her, it was gone from him forever. It was now late in the afternoon, and we were dismissed. Without saying a word to any one, Mr. Bill took his arithmatic and slate, (for ciphering, as it was called then, was his only study). We knew what it meant, for we felt, as well as he, that this was his last day at school. As my getting to school depended upon his continuance, I did not doubt that it was my last also.

On the way home, but not until after separating from all the other boys, Mr. Bill showed some disposition to boast.

'You all little fellows was monstous badly skeered this evening, Squire.'

'Was'nt you scared too?' I asked.

'Skeered? I'd like to see the schoolmaster that could skeer me. I skeered of Joe Larrabee?'

'I did not think you were scared of him,'

'Skeered of who then? Miss Larrabee? Old Red Eye? She mout be redder eyed than what she ar', and then not skeer me. Why look here, Squire, how would I look goin' into Dukesborough into Mr. Bland and Jones store, right from bein' skeered of old Miss Larrabee? To be runnin' right intoo Mr. Bland and Jone's store, and old Mehetibilly Larrabee right arter me, or old Joe nuther. It wur well for him that he never struck Betsy Ann Acry. Ef he had a struck her, Jo Larrabee's strikin' days would be over.'

'But was'nt you goin' to take her whippin' for her?'

'Lookee here, Squire, I didn't take it, did I?'

'No; but you said you was ready to take it.'

'Poor little fellow!' he said, compassionately. 'Squire, you are yit young in the ways of this sorrowful and ontimely world. Joe Larrabee knows me, and I knows Joe Larrabee, and as the feller said, that in' sufficient.'

We were now at our gate. Mr. Bill bade me good evening, and passed on and thus ended his pupilage and mine at the school of Josiah Lorriby.

MISS PEA, MISS SPOUTER AND THE YANKEE.

CHAPTER I.

"Companions
That do converse, and waste the time together,
Whose souls do bear an equal yoke of love."
Merchant of Venice.

Mr. Benjamin (but as everybody called him uncle Ben) Pea, resided two miles out of Dukesborough ; he was a small farmer—not
small in person, but a farmer on a small scale. He raised considerable corn, a trifle of cotton, great quantities of potatoes and some
pinders. It was said that in his younger days he used to be brisk in
his business and to make something by hauling wood to town. He
spent as little as he could and saved as much as he could ; but for a
certain purpose he kept as good an establishment as he could. His
little wagon used to be good enough to carry him and the old woman
to town, yet he bought a second hand gig, and did other things in
proportion. It was extravagant and he knew it, but he had a purpose. That purpose was to marry off his daughter Georgiana. Now,
Georgiana had told him for years and years, even before the old
woman died, that if he wanted to marry her off (a thing she cared
nothing about herself) the only way to do that was for the family to
go in a decent way. And now the old woman had died, and her
father had grown old, she had her own way, and that was as decent
as could be afforded, and no more.

Miss Georgiana Pea was heavy ; heavy of being married off, and
heavy of body ; her weight for fifteen years at the least, had not
been probably less than one hundred and seventy pounds. In her
seasons of highest health, which were probably oftener in the latter
part of the fall than at any other period of the year, people used to
guess that it might be even more ; but there was no getting at it at
any time, because she always stoutly refused to be weighed. True,
she laced, but that did not seem to diminish her materially, for what
was pressed down by the corsets managed to re-appear somewhere
else. She had a magnificent bust—this bust was her pride, that was

evident. Indeed, she as good as confessed as much to me. I knew
the family well : she did'nt mind me—I was a very small boy, and
she was aware that I considered that bust a wonderful work of
nature.

Yet she did'nt marry. The old gentleman had been so anxious
about it, that he had long ago rather given it out in a public way
that upon her marriage with his consent, (she was the only child—
Peterson died when a boy, of measles) he should give up everything,
houses, lands, stock furniture, and money, and live upon the bounty
of his son-in-law. These several items of property had been often
appraised by the neighbors as accurately as could be done, (considering that the exact amount of money could not be gotten at) in view
of ascertaining for their own satisfaction what her dowry might be.
The appraisement had gone through many gradations of figures, while
the bridegroom delayed his coming. At the period of which I am
now telling, there were those who maintained that uncle Ben was
worth four thousand dollars ; others shook their heads·and said
thirty-five hundred ; while others yet, who claimed to know more
about it than any body else, they did'nt care who it was, insisted that
three thousand was the outside. Many a man, it seemed to me, and
one that would have been worth having, might have been caught by
that bust and that prospective fortune. I remember that I was constantly expecting them to marry her off. But they did not ; and now,
at thirty, or thereabout, she was evidently of the opinion that even if
she had many desires to enter into the estate of marriage, their chances
of gratification were few. Indeed, Miss Pea was at that stage when
she was beginning to speak often of the other sex with disgust.

Mr. Jacob Spouter resided in the very heart of Dukesborough, and
kept a hotel. The town being small, his business was small. He
was a small man, but looked bright, capable and business like. To
look at him, you would have supposed that he kept a good hotel, but
he did not. It is surprising, indeed, to consider how few men there
are who do. But this is a great theme and entirely independent of
what I wish to tell, except so far as it may relate to the fact that Mr.
Spouter had yet living with him, an only child, a daughter, whose
name was Angeline. Miss Angeline, in short, took after the Fanigans,
who were long. She was a very thin young lady, almost too thin to
look well, and her hair and complexion were rather sallow. But then
that hair curled—every hair curled.

Who has not a weakness? Miss Pea had hers, we saw ; and now
we shall see, as everybody for years had seen, that Miss Spouter had
hers, also. It was an innocent one—it was her curls. In the memory of man that hair had never been done up, but through all changes
of circumstances and weather, it had hung in curls, just as it hung on
the day when this story begins. They had been complimented

thousands of times, and by hundreds of persons ; the guests of years had noticed them, and had uttered and smiled their approbation ; and there had been times when Miss Spouter hoped, in spite of the want of other as striking charms, and in spite of the universally known fact that her father had always been insolvent and always would be, that those curls would eventually entangle the person, without whom she felt that she never could be happy. While this person was a man, it was not any particular individual of the species. Many a time had she seen one who, she thought, would answer. She was not very fastidious, but she positively believed (and this belief made her appear to be anxious) that in view of all the circumstances of her life, the best thing that she could do for herself would be to marry ; besides, there was something in her, she thought, which she constantly understood to be telling her that if she had the opportunity, she could make some man extremely happy.

But though those curls had been so often praised—yea, though they had been sometimes handled—to such a degree did people's admiration of them extend, that Miss Spouter, like her contemporary in the country, was unmarried, and beginning to try to feel as if she despised the vain and foolish world of man.

These young ladies were friends and had been always. They were so much attached that each seemed, to a superficial observer, to believe that she had been born for but one special purpose, and that was to help the other to get married ; for Miss Spouter believed and Miss Pea knew that marriage was a subject which, without intermission, occupied the mind of her friend. It was pleasant to hear Miss Spouter, who was more sentimental and the l . . . r talker of the two, praise Miss Pea's 'figger,' by which terms she meant only her bust. No one ever dreamed that it was possible for any jealousy to rise between them ; for Miss Spouter had no figure worth mentioning, and not a hair of Miss Pea's head could be curled ; not only so, but the fact was, that in her heart of hearts (so curious a thing is even the most constant friendship) neither thought much of the other's special accomplishment ; rather, each thought that there was entirely too much of it, especially Miss Spouter touching the 'figger.' If Miss Pea considered the property qualification in her favor, Miss Spouter did not forget that she resided right in the very heart of Dukesborough, and that her father kept a hotel. Now, as long as the world stands, persons of their condition who live in town, will feel a little ahead of those who live in the country ; while the latter, though never exactly knowing why, will admit that it is so. Miss Pea was generally very much liked by the neighbors ; Miss Spouter had not made a great number of friends. Probably town airs had something to do in the matter. Miss Pea was considered the superior character of the two, but neither of them thought so ; Miss Spouter, especially, who knew the meaning of many more words in the dictionary than her friend, and who had read Alonzo and Melissa and the Three Spaniards, until she had the run of them fully, never dreamed of such a thing.

Miss Spouter was fond of visiting Miss Pea, especially in watermelon time. Miss Pea valued the friendship of Miss Spouter because it afforded her frequent opportunities of staying at a hotel, a privilege which she well knew not many country girls enjoy ed. To stay there, not as a boarder, but as a friend of the family; to eat there, and sleep there, and not to pay for either of these distinctions as other people did, but to do these things on invitation' Now, while Miss Pea got much better eating and sleeping at home yet she could but consider the former as privileges. She never would forget that once when there was a show in Dukesborough, given by a ventriloquist, who was also a juggler, she had been at Mr. J. Spouter's and had been introduced to the wonderful man and his wife too, and had heard them talk about general matters just as other people did.

But time was waxing old. The bust had about ceased to be ambitious, and the curls, though wishful yet, were falling into the habit of giving only despondent shakes.

CHAPTER II.

Miss Spouter sat in the hotel parlor ; it was on the first floor and opened upon the street ; in it were two wooden rocking-chairs, six split-bottoms and a half to and. I shall not undertake to describe the window-curtains. She was pensive and silent ; the still summer evening disposed her to meditation. She sat silent and pensive, but not gloomy. Looking out from the window, she espied on the further side of the square, Miss Pea, who was in the act of turning towards her. Here she came, in good yellow calico and a green calash. As she walked, her arms were crossed peacefully upon her chest.

'Howdye, stranger !' saluted Miss Spouter. They had not met in a fortnight.

'Stranger yourself,' answered Miss Pea, with a smile and a sigh. They embraced ; the curls fell upon the bust and the bust fostered the curls, as only long tried friends can fall upon and foster. Miss Pea came to stay all night ; never had they slept in the same house without sleeping together.

'Well, Georgy,' Miss Spouter remarked, sweetly, but almost invidiously, as they were getting into bed, 'figger is figger.'

'It's no sich a thing,' answered Miss Pea, with firm self denial ; 'it's curls, you know it's curls.'

'No, George, its figger.'

'Angeline Spouter, you know it aint ; its curls, and you know its curls.'

They blew out the candle, and for a short time continued this friendly discussion ; but soon Miss Pea got the best of it, as usual, and Miss Spouter, by silence and other signs, admitted that it was curls.

———

'We've been sleeping a long time together, George.'

'We have that.'

'Ten years.'

'Yes, fifteen of 'em.'

'Gracious me ! fifteen ?'

'Yes, indeed '

'Well, but I was but a child then.'

Miss Pea coughed. She was the elder by exactly six months.

'Did we think ten years ago that you would now be a Pea and I a Spouter ?'

'I did'nt think much about myself, but I had no idea you would.'

'Yet so it is ; you with your figger and yet a Pea.'

'And what is worse, you with your curls and yet a Spouter.'

'No, not worse. You ought to have been married years ago, Georgiana Pea.'

'If I had had your curls and had wanted to marry, *I should* a been married and forgot it.'

'No, George, I never had the requisite figger.'

'Angeline Spouter, do hush.'

———

'Suppose we had married, George ?'

'Well.'

'I think I could have made my husband love me as few men have ever loved, be they whomsoever they might.'

'Ah ! every body knows that.'

'No, alas ! none but thee, George.'

'Yes, but I know better.'

Miss Spouter again gave it up.

———

'Do you reckon we would have had families, George ?'

Miss Pea smothering her head under her friend's pillow, declared that she could laugh fit to kill herself.'

'I have often thought, my dear George, of what I would think if I had married, and had a little girl—'

'With curly hair ?'

'Well—yes ; I should have had no objection, but—I hope he would have been a good child, George.'

'No doubt about that,' answered Miss Pea, with something of a yawn.'

'She should have loved you, Georgiana, and all yours.'

'All mine ?' Miss Pea seemed to wake up.

'Yes, all yours.'

'Well, if I had been married, and if it had been my lot, I would'nt a wanted it to been but one, certain, sure.'

'And that should have been Georgiana Pea, over and over again.'

'Well, it should'nt ; he—'

'Ho ? O, George, would you have had a boy ? What a creature !'

'Yes, I would, Angy, certain ; girls are a trouble.'

'But girls are so much prettier, George,—la, me !'

'They may be prettier, but they are a trouble.'

'He would have been a good child, Georgy.'

'If he had'nt I'd have made him good.' Miss Pea spoke with decision.

'Oh, you cruel creature !'

'No, I'm not cruel, Angeline, but I belive in making children mind.'

'So do I, but I can't see how a woman can beat her own offspring to death.' Miss Spouter was indignant.

'I don't mean that ; still—la, Angeline Spouter, what are we talkin about ? we have'nt got any children, and as for me, I shall never have any myself, certain and sure !'

Miss Pea laughed heartily, but Miss Spouter sighed, and remarked that it was not in people to say what was to be nor what was'nt to be.'

———

'George, I do believe you are going to sleep.'

Miss Pea declared that she was'nt, and like all persons of her size, she thought she was telling the truth. Miss Spouter had one or two other remarks which she always made on such occasions, and which she wanted to make now.'

'Georgiana Pea, do you or do you not ever expect to marry ? I ask you candidly.'

'No, Angeline, I don't ; I may have had thoughts, I may have had expectations ; pap looks as if he would go distracted if I don't marry, but to tell you the truth, I have about come to the conclusion that there's more marries now than does well. Pap declares that he means to marry me off to somebody before he dies. He thinks that I could'nt take care of myself if he was to die, and that he takes care of me now himself. I think I'm the one that takes care of him, and I think I could take as good care of myself then as I do now. He says I shall marry though, and I'm waitin to see how it'll be. But I tell you, Angeline Spouter, that there's more marries now than ever does well.

'And—well,' answered Miss Spouter, 'and so have I concluded about it. It is the honest expression of the genuine sentiments of my innermost heart. What is man? A deceitful, vain and foolish creature, who will to-day talk his honey words, and praise a girl's curls, and to-morrow, he is further off than when we first laid our eyes on him. What is your opinion of man, George? What now is your opinion of Tom Dyson, who used to melt before the sight of you like butter ere the sun had set?'

'I think of Tom Dyson like I think of Barney Bolton who used to praise your curls just like they were so much gold, and like I think of all of 'em, and that's about as much as I think of a old dead pine tree or post oak.'

Miss Pea had not read many books like Miss Spouter, and must necessarily, therefore, borrow her comparisons from objects familiar to her country life. Miss Spouter noticed the difference, but refrained from remarking on it.

'And yet, Georgiana, there is something in me, I feel it; it tells me that I could have made Barney Bolton much happier than Malinda Jones has. Barney Bolton is not happy, Georgiana Pea.'

Miss Pea only coughed.

Yes, indeed! Alas! I see it in his eye; I see it in his walk; I see it in his every action. The image of Angeline Spouter is in his breast and it will stay there forever.'

Miss Pea was always perfectly silent, and endeavored to feel solemn when this last speech was said.

'If you were to marry, George, I should be the *lonesomest* creature in the wide, wide world.'

'Ah, well! when I marry, which is never going to be the case, (that is exceptin pap do go distracted and hunt me up a good chance) you'll be married and forget it, and that little curly headed girl will be readin, ritin and cypherin.' Miss Pea yawned and laughed slightly.

'Never, never! But won't you let your little boy come sometimes in a passing hour to see a lonesome girl, who once was your friend, but now, alas! abandoned?'

'Angeline Spouter, do hush.

* * * * *. *

'George, it is very warm to-night; is it late?'

'I should think it was,' answered Miss Pea, and snored.

Miss Spouter lay for some time awake, but silent. She then lifted the curtain from the window through which the moon, high in heaven, shone upon the bed, withdrew from her cap five or six curls, extending them upon her snowy breast, smiled dismally, put them up again, looked a moment at her companion, then abruptly turned her back to her, and went to sleep.

CHAPTER III.

"Is all the counsel that we too have shared,
The sisters' vows, the hours that we have spent
When we have chid the hasty footed time
For parting us----O, and is all forgot?"
                              Midsummer-Night's Dream.

But friendship, like other good things, has enemies. One of the most dangerous of these is a third person. These beings are among the most inconvenient and troublesome upon earth. Not often do confidential conversations take place in a company of three, especially conversations appertaining to friendship or love. When sentiments, hot from the heart, has to move in triangles, it must often meet with hindrances and cool itself before it has reached its destination. As in mathematics, between two points, so in social life between two hearts; the shortest way is a straight line. A third person makes a divergence and a delay. Third persons have done more to separate very friends and lovers, than all the world besides. They had gotten between other persons before, and now, one of them had come to get between Miss Spouter and Miss Pea.

Adiel Slack, some years before, had left his native Massachusetts, and from going to and fro upon the earth, came in an evil day, and put up at the inn of Jacob Spouter. He was tall, deep voiced, big footed, and the most deliberate looking man that had ever been in Dukesborough. He was one of those imperturbable Yankees that could fool you when you were watching him just as well as when you were not. When he said that he was twenty-eight his last birth-day, his fresh looking hair, his unwrinkled and unblushing cheek, and his entire freedom from all signs of wear and care, made one believe that it must be so. If he had said that he was forty-five, the gravity of his countenance, the deliberation of his gait, and the deep, wordly wisdom of his eye would have made one believe that he spoke truly.

The mere arrival of such a person in that small community, must necessarily create some stir. He was greatly the most remarkable one of all the passengers who came by that morning's stage. While they ate their breakfast with that haste which is peculiar to the traveling public, he took his time. The stage went away and left him at the table eating his fifth biscuit, while Mrs. Spouter's eyes were fixed upon him with that steadfast look with which she was wont to regard all persons who ate at her table more than she thought was fair. He took another biscuit, looked about for more butter and attempted to open a conversation with that lady; but she was not in the mood to be communicative, so he set to the work of studying her. He made her out to be a woman of a serious turn of mind, less attentive to dress than her husband, but at the same time aspiring and possibly with propriety and with success to be the head of

the family. After breakfast, he stood about, sat about, picked his
teeth, ('with a ivory lancet, blamed if it were'nt,' Mr. Spouter said)
then took his hat and strolled about the village all the forenoon.
He went into both the stores, got acquainted with the doctor and the
black smith, and the shoemaker, found and bargained for the rent of
a room, and at dinner, announced himself a citizen of Georgia and a
merchant of Dukesborough. In less than a week, a small stock of
goods had arrived and were neatly arranged in the room, over the
door of which, hung a sign board, painted by himself, which made
Mr. Boggs and Messrs. Bland and Jones wish either that they had
never had sign boards, or that Adiel Slack, dry goods merchant, had
never come there.

Being a single man, Mr. Slack boarded at the hotel of J. Spouter.
Now, no sooner was it settled that he was to become a citizen than
Miss Spouter, according to ancient usage in such cases, felt herself
to be yielding to the insidious influences of yet another love. Who
knew, she thought, that the fond dream of her life was not destined now to become a blissful consummation. The fact that Mr.
Slack had come from afar, made her sentimental soul only the more
hopeful. How this was so she could not tell, but it was so, and the
good girl began at once to bestow the most assiduous cultivation
upon every charm which she thought she possessed. Mr. Slack soon
began to be treated with more consideration than any of the boarders. He had within a week moved from Mr. Spouter's end of the
table up to Mrs. Spouter's, an become, as it were, that lady's left
bower, Miss Angeline being, of course, her right. The hot biscuit
were always handed first to him, and if anybody got a hot waffle, it
was he. People used to look up towards Mrs. Spouter and get occasional glimpses of little plates of fresh butter and preserves that
tried to hide behind the castors or the candlestick. When there was
pie, Mr. Slack was helped first, because, among other things, he was
the more sure of getting another piece, if the pie, as it sometimes
would happen, in spite of precaution, should not go around the
second time.

The servants did not like him because he never gave them a kind
word nor a cent of money. But let any one of them omit to hand
the best things to him first. O, the partiality that was shown as
plain as day to that man! Every body saw it, and spoke of it
among confidential friends. Some said it was a sin ; some said it
was a shame, and some went so far as to say it was both.

Among the boarders, was one whom we have seen before. For
Mr. Bill Williams had now been installed in his office, and had
already began to take new responsibilities. When this conduct
towards the new comer had become notorious, he was heard by
many persons even to swear that he'd be dinged of he had had a hot

waffle, even when thar was waffles, sen c that dadblasted Yankee had
moved up to old Miss Spouter's eend. As for the second piece of
pie, he had done gin out ever hearin of the like any mor throout the
ages of a sorrowful and ontimely world.' He spoke with feeling it
is true ; but he was a clerk in Mr. Bland's store, and he thought
that if he could not take some responsibility, the question was who
could. 'Consequenses mout be consequences,' said Mr. Bill, 'be they
now or at some fater day. I takes the responsibility to say that the
case ar a onfair, and a imposition on the boarders and on the tran-
shent people, and it war also a shame on Dukesborough, and also
——,' Mr. Bill shook his head for the conclusion.

But in spite of every body and every thing, Mr. Slack kept his
place. He soon discovered Miss Spouter's weakness and her pa-
sion. Flattering as it might be to find himself the favored object of
her pursuit, yet the reflection that her only capital was a head of
curls, which in time would fade, caused him to determine, after making
his calculations, that no profit was to be netted in being caught. It
was not to be overlooked, however, that there would be, if not an
entire saving of expense, at least a postponement of its payment in
keeping his thoughts to himself and in seeming to be drawing nearer
and nearer the vortex which was ready to swallow him up. The
terms of board at Mr. Spouter's included monthly payments. These
did not suit calculations which were made upon the principle of col-
lecting his own dues at once and postponing his payments as long
as possible, and if possible, to the end of time. Now, he guessed
that great as were Mr. Spouter's needs, that affectionate father would
not be the man to run the risk of driving off his daughter's suitor
by worrying him with dues for a little item of board, which might all
come back again into the family. In addition to this, he was not
insensible to the advantage of maintaining his seat at the dinner
table, where biscuits, waffles and pies, when they came at all, were
wont to make their first appearance. These several matters, being
actual money to him, were not to be overlooked by a man who did
nothing without deliberation. After deliberating, therefore, he determined to so conduct himself before the Spouters as to create the
hope that the time would come when he would solicit the hand of
her who long had been willing to bestow it upon somebody. But
he was careful to keep his own advances and his meetings of advances without the pale of such contingences as he had named were,
in the South, accustomed to follow breaches of marriage contracts.
He maintained his place at the table, and took what it afforded, in
the manner of a man who was very near to being one of the family.
He chatted in a very familiar manner with Mrs. Spouter, and sym-
pathised with her and Mr. Spouter's complaints of the high price of
everything except board. He lounged in the parlor, where he told

to Miss Angeline touching stories of his boyhood's home. He bestowed due admiration upon those curls which, every time he saw them, reminded him of a portrait of his mother, (now a saint in heaven) taken when she was a girl eighteen years old. Then he spoke feelingly of how he had been a wanderer, and how he began to think it was time he had settled himself for good ; how he had never felt exactly ready for that until since he had come to Dukesborough, and that—and that—and that—— embarrassment would prevent him from saying more. But whenever he got to this point, and Miss Angeline's heart would be about to burst, and she would be getting ready to cast herself upon his faithful bosom, he would change abruptly, become frightened, go away and stay away for a week.

At their first meeting at the breakfast table after such scenes, Miss Spouter would appear quite conscious, hold herself yet straighter and endeavor to show that she had spirit. But before she had carried it far, she would conclude to stop where she was, go back and begin again.

CHAPTER IV.

But while these things were going on among the Spouters, what had become of the Peas ? who ever supposes that Miss Georgiana was buried in the country, dead or alive, is simply mistaken. When she heard that there was a new store in town, she wanted to see it ; and when uncle Ben heard that it was kept by a bachelor, he was determined that he should see his daughter : for as he grew older, his anxiety became more intense for Georgiana to find some body, as he expressed it, 'to take keer of her when my head gits cold.' He begged her several times to go before she was ready.

'Georgy, put on your yaller caliker and go long.'

'Pap, do wait till I get ready. ' I do believe you will go distracted.'

Georgiana waited until she got ready, and when she did get ready she went. Her plan was to go and spend the night with Miss Spouter, and in company with her visit the new store the next morning.

Some persons believe in presentiments, and some do not. I hardly know what to think of such things, and have never yet made up my mind whether they are reliable or not. Sometimes they seem to foreshadow coming events, and sometimes they are clearly at fault. I have occasionally had dre s, and subsequent events were in such exact accordance with i that I have been inclined to accord to them much of the importance that by some persons it is maintained they have. Then, again, t dreams I have had (for I have always been a dreamer) have be. entirely unreasonable, nay, absurd, and even ridiculous, as to be impossible of fulfillment. For instance, I have more than once dreamed that I was a woman, and I have since been much amused by the recollection of some of the silly things that I did and said while in that estate. I do not consider this an opportune place to mention them, even if they were worthy of mention on any occasion, and I allude to them for the purpose of saying that after such dreams I have been disposed to reject the whole of the theory of dreams.

But all this is neither here nor there. The divergence from my story, though natural, cannot with propriety be farther extended, and I will return at once to my two heroines in whose deportment immediately subsequent to what was last being done by them both, will be found the reason why such divergence was made.

No sooner had Miss Spouter determined fully in her mind that she would catch Mr. Slack if she could, than she was conscious of a wavering in her friendship for Miss Pea; for she felt that that person was destined to be the greatest, if not the only barrier between her and the object of her pursuit. She, Miss Spouter, had seen him first she thought. She had, as it were, found him, and when George was not even looking for any such property. George did not have even a shadow of the remotest claim to him. It was wrong and unkind in George to interfere. She, Miss Spouter, wouldn't have treated her so. Now all this was before Miss Pea had ever laid eyes on Mr. Slack, and Miss Spouter knew it. That made no difference, she said to herself, if anything, it made it worse. She was hurt and she could not help it.

Miss Pea might have had a presentiment of this state of things, and she might not. But at all events, when she went upon her visit, she carried a bucket of butter as a present to Mrs. Spouter. It was just before supper time, and consequently too late for her to return that evening. If it had not been, as she afterwards declared upon her word and honor, she would have done so. The Spouters were as cold as ice. Not even the bucket of butter could warm Mrs. Spouter a single degree. Strange conduct for her. Miss Angeline at first thought that she would not go in to the supper table. But then that would be too plain, and upon reflection, she thought she preferred to be there.

Miss Pea and Mr. Slack, of course, had to be introduced. He found her disposed to be chatty. Miss Spouter looked very grave; and raised her pocket handkerchief to her mouth, as an occasional provincialism fell from the lips of her country visitress, while her dear mother, taking the cue, would glance slyly at Mr. Slack and snicker.

'This is uncommon good butter, Mrs. Spouter,' he remarked to the lady of the house; and oh, the quantities of butter that man did consume!

Now, it was from Miss Pea's bucket; they did not like to confess it, but they had it to do.

'Ah? Oh! well, Miss Pea's mother must be a noble housekeeper.' Mrs. Pea had been dead several years.

'Is it possible? You, then!'

Miss Georgiana would have told a lie if she had not acknowledged that it was.

Mr Slack bestowed a look of intense admiration upon her which made Miss Spouter become quite grave, and her mother somewhat angry.

After supper the gentleman followed the ladies into the parlor. Miss Spouter was pensive, and complained of head-ache. Miss Pea did not believe she had it, and therefore she spoke freely of her father's plantation, of what he was to her and she to him, and of how he was always urging her to get married, a thing which she had made up her mind never to do. When they retired for the night, Miss Spouter being no better, but rather worse, they did what they had never done in their lives before, they slept apart. This was capping the climax, and Miss Pea went home the next morning, asking herself many times on the way, if friendship was anything but a name.

It seemed to be a sad thing that these young ladies should part. Hand in hand they had traveled the broad road of life, and never jostled each other when men were plentiful. But these animals had broken from them like so many wild cattle, some dodging and darting between them, some taking to by-paths, and some wildly leaping over precipices, until now they were drawing nigh to the road of young womanhood, and there was but one left for them both. If they could have divided him it might have been well; but he was indivisible. The fact is, Mr. Slack ought never to have come there, or he ought to have brought his twin brother with him.

'What's become of your friend?' he inquired at breakfast.

'She's gone to look after what she calls her father's plantation, I reckon,' answered Mrs. Spouter, sharply.

'Haint her father got any plantation, then?'

'He's got a little bit of two hundred acres of tolerably poor land. That's all the plantation he's got.'

'Oh, ma!' interceded Miss Angeline, 'Georgiana is a very good girl.'

'She may be good, but if you call her a gal I don't know what you would call them that's fifteen or twenty years younger; and if she was young that wouldn't make her daddy rich.'

'Oh, no! But, oh, ma!' Miss Spouter persisted in a general way, for she seemed to think that this was all that could be said in her

favor. Upon reflection she asked Mr. Slack if he did not think Miss
Pea had a good figger. Then she took a very small sip of water,
wiped her mouth carefully and coughed slightly.

'Wall, I—ah,' began Mr. Slack, but ma laughed so immoderately
that he laughed too, and did not finish giving his opinion in words.
Alas, for Miss Pea! Big as she was, she was cut all to pieces and
salted away by Mrs. Spouter, while Miss Angeline could only look
a little reproachfully now and then, and say 'Oh, ma."

*   *   *   *   *   *   *   *   *

'Two hundred acre.,' mused Mr. Slack on his bed that night. In
Massachusetts that is a considerable farm; other property in proportion. What would it bring in ready money if the old gentleman (he
is old, certain) should take a notion to give it up *now*; already some
money. He brought me a fine watermelon this morning, and asked
me to go out and see them all. I'm a going. Quick work, Adiel,
quick work,'

Mr. Slack was a hard man to catch; it had been tried before and
had failed. Nevertheless, Mrs. Spouter and Miss Spouter, about
six weeks later, actually caught him in the act of coming away
from Mr. Pea's· What made it worse, he had a bunch of pinks in
his hand. The next time Miss Spouter met Miss Pea, she did not
speak to her. She only shook her curls and said to herself in words
which were audible, 'such is life.' Georgiana folded her hands over
her bosom and asked, if friendship was not a name, what was it?

But the man maintained his place at the table, to which he march-
ed with unusual confidence and good humor at the first meal after
his detection; what is more, the little plates maintained their places.
In spite of all his goings to the Pea's and his returning with bunches
of pinks in his hands, his deportment in any other respect, had not,
at least for the worst, changed. Indeed, he looked oftener and
more proudly at the curls. Yes, thought Miss Spouter, he may
marry her, but the image of Angeline Spouter is in his breast, and
it will stay there forever. But for her entreaties her ma would have
removed the little plates and sent him back to the other end of the
table, where he came from.

'I'm jest the woman to do it,' she said. 'That long-legged Yankee has eat more than his worth in butter alone. The house 'll
break or be eat up, it makes no difference which, and nary cent of
money has he paid yit. Settle hisself, indeed! He'll never settle
his nasty self excipt whar thar's money, or everlastin butter, and
he not to pay for it neither. And I'll move them plates tu-morro
mornin, if I don't you may——'

'Oh, ma! he DON'T love her, I know he don't. Let them stay a
while longer.'

And the next morning the little plates would come in, take their places and look as cheerful as if nothing had happened.

Mr. Slack did a cash business. Time rolled on; the faster it rolled the cheaper he sold. His stock dwindled, and everybody asked why it was not being replenished. It began to be rumored that he was going to buy a plantation and settle himself. The rumor was traced to uncle Ben Pea. Miss Georgiana was asked about it and became confused.

'She jist as well a give it up,' said Mr. Bill Williams, at Mr. Spouter's table. Mr. Bill was gradually edging up towards 'quality eend' as he termed the head. 'In fac, she did give it up farly. I axed her a plain question; she couldn't say nothin, and she didn't. She merrily hung her head upon her bres, and she seem monsous comfortubble. She ar evidently scogitatin on the blessed joys of a futur state.'

The next morning, the little plates were absent, and Mr. Slack, without seeming to not' that Mr. Bill Williams had usurped his place, took his seat by M. 'pouter and talked with him in the manner of a man who had been on a journey of some weeks and had now returned. That g. leman did not seem to be at all congratulatory on the occasion, but immediately after, breakfast brought within view of his guest an amount for three months' board. The latter looked over it carefull, remarked that he thought it was correct, begged that it might be considered as cash, and walked away. This was an eventful day to Mr. Slack, for besides the aforementioned incident, he sold out the remainder of his stock to Messrs. Bland and Jones, went without his dinner, borrowed a gig from the Justice of the Peace, took him along with him to Mr Pea's, where, at three o'clock P. M. he was married to Miss Georgiana.

'Wretched creature!' exclaimed Angelina, the forsaken, when her mother informed her of the news at night. At first she thought she would faint; but she did not. She retired to her room, undressed, looked at her curls in the glass, even longer than was her wont, put them away tenderly, got into bed, apostrophised property and the other sordid things of this world, and went to sleep with this thought upon her mind: 'Georgiana Pea may be by his side, but the image of Angeline Spouter is in his breast, and it will stay there forever.

CHAPTER V.

"Are we not one? Ar we not joined by Heaven?"
Fair Penitent.

Georgiana was married and her father was satisfied. It was what he had wished a long time. The danger of going distracted was

100

HUMOROUS TALES.

over. He would have preferred a Southern man, it is true, but all of that class had discovered such a want to appreciate his Georgy that he persuaded himself that she had made a narrow escape in not marrying one of them. Mr. Slack had some ways of doing and talking that he did not quite understand; but he believed that they would wear off. Georgy now had a husband to take care of her when his head got cold, and that was enough. She did not seem to be perfectly happy, but, on the contrary, somewhat ill at ease. But then she wasn't any young thing to let getting married run her raving distracted. He liked Mr. Slack upon the whole; he suited him well enough, and that is what parents generally care mostly for. He was a business man, that's what he was. He talked upon business even on the afternoon of his marriage, and renewed the subject after supper and the next morning. One would have thought, to hear him talk about business, that the honey moon had shone out and gone down long ago. It did not look exactly right; but now, that Mr. Slack was a married man, he was for making something. If he owned the farm, he should do this thing and that thing, sell this piece of property and convert it into cash; in short, he should sell out the whole concern and go where land was cheaper and better. If it were left to him he should turn it over, so that in twelve months it should be worth at least twice as much as it was now. It was very clear to uncle Ben that his son-in-law was a business man; still, he did not make out the title deeds. Notwithstanding his hints to that effect heretofore, he had never entertained the slightest notion of such a thing. When Mr. Slack persisted in saying what he should do if he were the owner, the old gentleman took occasion to say, but in a somewhat jocose way, that he and Georgy would have to wait for that until his head got cold, which, he said by way of consoling for the disappointment, wouldn't be much longer. This was only a day or two after the marriage. Mr. Slack seemed to be somewhat hurt, but he merely remarked that he had a plenty to live on, and that all he wanted with property was for Georgiana to enjoy it. He had money enough to buy a tract of land adjoining Mr. Pea's and two or three fellows. If Georgiana had a good house woman it would save her from a good deal of work which now, since she was his wife, he would rather she didn't have to do; but—ah—he supposed he should have to wait for that.

Yes, but he needn't to do any such thing, Mr. Pea stoutly maintained. Those being Mr. Slack's intentions the 'oman should be bought. The money was there in that side-board drawer whenever they found one to suit them. He should buy the 'oman himself. The son-in-law's countenance brightened a little. He might have to go to Augusta in a few days; the likeliest gangs were there generally, and it might suit just as well to take the money along with him and buy the woman there. Georgiana didn't say anything ; but la me, what did she know about business ?

Mr. Slack sent into the village every day for the mail, for Dukesborough being immediately on the great line of travel, had its daily mail. He had been married less than a week, when, one morning a letter was brought to him which made him turn a little pale. Upon his father-in-law's inquiry from whence it came, he answered after a moment's hesitation, that it was from a man who owed him some money, and who had written to say that if he would meet him the next day in Augusta, he would pay him a hundred dollars and renew the note. A hundred dollars indeed ! The rascal had promised to pay half the note, and now as he was about settling himself he was to be put off with a hundred dollars. He had a good mind not to go and would not but for the importance of having the note renewed. But *could* he get there in time ? How was that Mr. Pea ? Why, it was easy enough ; the stage would pass in a couple of hours, and as it traveled all night, he could reach Augusta by nine o'clock the next morning. Mr. Slack hesitated. He was loth to go so soon after being married, but as he had expected to go in a few days any how, he guessed he had as well to go on at once, especially as negroes seemed to be rising in price, and it was important to get the woman as soon as possible. Certainly business was business, if people were married. Mr. Slack ought to go at once ; he should if it was him.

Uncle Ben took out the money, and Georgiana ordered lunch. Mr. Slack had so often complained of the old gentleman's time piece, that the latter, upon his entreaties to be allowed to take it with him for repairs (at no expense to the owner of course) consented. The man of business then went to packing his trunk and satchel. Although he was to stay but three days at furthest, yet, not knowing but that he might need them, he packed in all his clothes, looking about all over the house to be sure that he had not mislaid anything.

It was a nice lunch. It ought to have been, for it took a long time to be gotten ready. Mr. Slack was not sure that he was going to get his supper, and he therefore determined to put away enough to last him to the end of his journey. He had barely finished when the servant, who had been stationed to watch for the stage, announced that it was coming. He bade both an affectionate adieu, looked into the stage to see if there was any person in it whom he knew, didn't seem to be disappointed that there was not, hopped in, and off he went.

Far from pining on account of the absence of her mate, Georgiana, sensible woman that she was, went about her work as cheerfully as if nothing had happened. She had been so taken up with Mr. Slack that several small domestic matters needed to be put to rights again, and she seemed to be even glad of the opportunity to look after them. She actually sang at her work—she was a good singer, too. The Pees always had been; I knew the family well. She wasn't going to fret herself to death, certain and sure. So she resumed her old tasks and habits, moved things back to their old places, and, in every respect, did as if she had forgotten that she had ever been married.

Uncle Ben was glad to see her in such gay spirits. He knew what it was all for, and he laughed inwardly and became gay himself. It was that nigger 'oman. The old man counted ten days and nights. As much as he wanted to see Mr. Slack, he wanted yet more to see his watch; without it he felt like a man without a newly amputated leg. But that, he would not allow to trouble him very much. He talked a great deal, especially at meal times about his Georgy's prospects, joked her about many things, talked of the prospects again and what he and Mr. Slack were going to do to make her the happiest woman in the world. Georgiana never suggested any change of their plans, and looked as if she intended to be but clay in their hands.

Three days passed. Mr. Slack's very longest time was out. The stage hove in view: Mr. Pea was at his gate, his hat was in his hand.

'Good mornin, uncle Ben,' said the driver, and was passing on.

'Hello! hello, Thompson,' shouted the old man. Thompson drew up

'Haint you got Mr. Slack aboard?'

'No, sir!'

'Haint you got a nigger 'oman?'

'No, sir.'

'Whar's Mr. Slack?'

'I don't know.'

'Haint you seed him?'

'No, sir.'

'Haint you hearn of him?'

'No, sir.'

'Why, what upon yearth does it mean?

Mr. Slack didn't go to nary tavern, but got off at a privit 'ouse way up town. I haint seed him nor heern from him sence. Was he to get back to-night?'

'Why, yes, certain and sure without fail.'

Well, he aint here, certin. Good evenin.'

'Is haint come, Georgy,' said uncle Ben, as he went into the house.

'Is he?'

'Why, no, he haint.'

Well, we must fry and wait till he does come '

Uncle Ben was too much occupied with his own disappointment to observe the equanimity with which Georgy bore her's. It was now bed time; the daughter went to her room, the father sat up at least half an hour longer than usual. He was disappointed, certain and sure. When people told people they were coming at a certain time, he wanted 'em to come; especially when they had people's watches. Oh, how he had missed it! If he had missed it by day he had missed it as much by night. It used to hang by a nail over his bed, and he longed for the gentle lullaby of its tickings. He had to go to bed, of course, but he lay awake another half an hour. A dreadful thought came: What if Mr. Slack, after all, was an IMPOSTEREE! Oh, he couldn't bear it. So he turned over and went to sleep; but it wouldn't stay behind, it crawled over and came close to him in his sleep, and he dreamed that he was the owner of a jeweler's shop, and that while he had no power to move, thieves were breaking through and stealing.

The next morning, immediately after breakfast, uncle Ben stood at his gate. He had a notion that Mr. Slack was coming in a private conveyance. Sure enough, yonder came a gig with a man in it and a horse behind with something on the horse. Uncle Ben's eyes were dim, and he couldn't make it out; but he hoped and believed that it was a nigger 'oman. Vain hope and vain belief! The gig carried Mr. Triplet, the deputy Sheriff, and the horse bore Mr. Pucket, a young lawyer from town. Uncle Ben had no business with them, certain and sure; so he bade them a good morning, as they came up, and again turned his eyes up the road. But the gentlemen stopped, and inquired if Mr. Slack was at home, No, but Mr. Pea looked for him every instant. He had been gone to Augusty three days, and was to a been back last night, but he didn't.

Mr. Triplet looked upon Mr. Pucket and smiled; Mr. Pucket looked upon Triplet, but did not smile.

'You must follow him.'

'There must some foller him that kin run faster than I kin.' answered Mr. Triplet.

'Foller who?' asked Mr. Pea.

'Mr. Slack.'

'Why he'll be here to-night. Or I'll be bound he's in a private conveyance, and'll be here this mornin. In cose he's comin back; becase he's got four hundred dollars of my money to buy a nigger 'oman with, and my watch besides. In cose he's comin back.'

Mr. Triplet looked upon Mr. Pea and smiled compassionately. Mr. Pea looked upon Mr. Triplet and frowned threatningly.

'What's the matter, Jim Triplet?,

'The matter ar, that you won't see your four hundred dollars agin, nor your watch, nor the gentleman what carried 'em off.'

'Why, what upon yearth is you talkin about.

'I ar talkin about the business of my office, which 'ar to arre 'Mr. Adad Slack, or Mr. Elisha Lovejoy, or Mr. Ephraim Hamlin, or what mout be the name of the gentleman that carried off your four hundred dollars and your watch.'

'Don't kick before you're spurred, Triplet, because nobody aint accused him of takin the money and watch—leastways of stealin it. Mr. Slack is a honest man and my son-in-law, and I tell you he'll be back to-night, and I look for him every minit of the day.'

So much the better for us if he do come. I has not come to arre s him for taking of the money and the watch, which is misdemeanors that I didn't know of tell now. But he is charge of obtainin credit by false pretensions, of stealin divers money, of tradin with niggers, and finally, with marryin three wimming, and not waitin for nary one of 'em to die fust.'

'Oh, Lordy!' exclaimed Mr. Pea. He then approached the sheriff, and in a tone which invited candor and confidence, and even hinted at gratitude, said,

'Jeems Triplet, I voted for you, you know I did; I always has. Ar what you say a fac?'

'I know you did, uncle Ben, and I tell you the plain truth, it ar a fac. Thay aint no doubt about it. Mr. Pucket here can tell you all about it.'

Mr. Pea, without waiting to hear further, turned and got into the house as fast as he could. He went into a shed room with uncommon desperation for a man of his years, and raised his hands in order to take down a shot gun from two forks on which it used to hang. The forks were there, but the gun was gone. He looked at the forks with the most resentful astonishment, and with a voice towering with passion, asked them what in the name of thunder had become of his gun? Not receiving any answer, he put the same interrogatory to the corner behind the door, to the space under the bed, and even to two small glass drawers, after opening and shutting them with great violence. He then ran back to the front door and questioned the whole universe on the subject.

'ROBBED! ROBBED!!' roared the old man. 'Gen-tul-men, ef I aint robbed, ——.' Mr. Pea had not 'cussed' before (as he afterwards declared upon his word and honor) in twenty years.

'Georgy! Where's Georgy?' It just now occurred to him that it was possible that Georgy might not like the state of things herself.

Georgiana had been at the dairy, superintending her butter. She had seen the men as they came, had gone into the house as quietly as she could and was peeping and listening through the window of her own room.

'Pap,' she said, not loudly, but earnestly, 'do come here, if you please.'

He went into her room.

'I reckon now you're satisfied. He's got what he came here for; he's stole from you, and he's stole from me; I haint a pocket handkerchief to my name. But do, for goodness' sake, go and send them men away.'

'Oh, Lordy!' reiterated Mr. Pea, retiring. 'Gen-tul-men, its no use, we are cotcht; Georgy and me has both been cotcht—I acknowledge the corn; and what is worser, it seem that I am the cause of it all. He have took my money, he have took my watch, he have took my gun, and da-ing his low life skin, he have even took Georgy's pocket handkerchiefs. It seem like he jest picked me and Georgy out for all his rascalities. And to think that I should be cused for it all. I *did* want her to marry. It look like a pity for her not to git married. And now she is married, and what have she married? A nasty, da-dblasted thievious Yankee, and aint even married at that. She is married and she aint married; and I don't understand it; and ef there's conchekenches, thay aint nobody can tell what it will be; and Georgy's name will go down to posterity, and the Peas wont be nobody any more; and—Oh, Lordy!'

'Pap, do for goodness gracious' sake, hush and come in the house,' said Georgiana, advancing to the front door. 'The Lord knows I'm glad I aint married; and if 'them other women don't grieve after him any more than I grieve after him, they've done forgot him, that's all. Pap, do come in the house.'

Mr. Pea subsided, and the men rode away. Mr. Pucket begged Mr. Trip-let to hasten, but the latter, who was too old to be running for nothing, de-clared in round terms that he'd be dinged ef he did.

'I wouldn't a made myself ridiculous, Pap, before company, if I'd a been in your place. That was pretty talk to have before men, and I in the house hearin every word.'

Mr. Pea, hearing himself accused of a new crime, couldn't stand it.'

'I do believe that if old Satan was to come, it would be me that fotch him, or leastways sent for him, and I'd as leave he had a come as that d-adblasted Yankee. Yes, its me, in case its me.' Anything wrong, I done it; oh, yes, in case, certing. Whar's my hat?' And the good man sallied forth to his field, where he remained until dinner time. There were so many contending emotions in his breast that he ate in silence. Georgiana had a good appetite; she ate away with a gusto and eyed her father amusedly.

'Pap, if I ll tell you something will you swear you'll keep it .

Uncle Ben laid down his knife and fork and gazed at her in amazement

'Wipe your mouth, Pap, and tell me if you'll swear.

'What is it ?' he demanded authoritatively.

'Will you swear, I asked you?'

'That's a mighty pooty question for a child to ask its parent.

'Oh, very well.' And she helped herself again from her favorite dish

'Won't you have some more, pap?'

'Georgy, what does you mean?'

'Will you swear?'

'No, I wont.'

'Oh, very well then.' And she peppered and salted.

'Well, I never 'spected to come to this while my head was hot. My own child, that I've raised, and raised respectable, to be settin thar, at my own table, a axin her own parrent to swar, jist the same as of I was gwine into a Free Mason's lodge, which she knows I don't hold with no sich.'

'Pap, I've heard you often talkin against the Free Uasons. I never thought they were so mighty bad. What do they do that is so awful bad?'

'You don't do you? No, I suppose you don't : in cose you don t, takin arter them as you do, in cose you don't.'

'How do I take after 'em ?'

'In havin o' secrets that's a sin to keep, and in tryin to make people . war that they won't tell 'em, and not even to their own parrents. That's how you are takin arter them.'

'Oh, yes, I see now,' she said, appearing to muse. 'Still this is something that I couldn't tell without your swearing not to mention to a blessed soul. Its worth swearin for, pap.'

'Ar it anything concerning that mean runaway Yankee?'

'If it is will you swear ?'

'Yes, I WILL, and cuss too, if you want me. I've been a cussin to myself all day any how.'

'You've cussed to other people besides yourself, but I only want you to swear.'

She brought the family Bible.

'La, Georgy, is you in yearnest sure enough ? Why, what do you mean ? You aint no Jestice.'

It made no difference ; she made him place his hand on the book and swear that he would never reveal what she was going to tell him without her consent. Uncle Ben was very solemn while the oath was being administered.

It required several minutes to impart the secret. 'The old man's joy was boundless. He jumped up and ran into his own room, where he cut up more capers than any one could have believed that he could cut up; he ran back again, made Georgiana rise from the table, hugged her, and made her sit down again; he rushed to the front door and huzzaed to the outer world; he rushed back again and hugged Georgy as she sat. Then he took his seat again and looked upon her with ineffable admiration. Suddenly he grew serious.

'Oh, Georgy' no if I only had——'

Before he could speak' further she taken something from her bosom, and handed it to him. He seized it with both hands, gazed at it, held it at arm's length and gazed at it. opened and looked into it, shut it up again, held it for a moment to his ear. patted it gently, laid it on the table, then lifted up his voice and wept.

CHAPTER VI.

"I grant I am a woman."
Julius Cæsar.

When the news of Mr. Slack's escapade reached Dukesborough, there was running to and fro; business was suspended. Some asked if the like had ever been heard of. Others asked every body if they hadn't told him so. J. Spouter was among the former, and Mr. Bill Williams among the latter. He got leave of absence from the store in order to roam up and down all the forenoon, for the purpose of proving that he had prophesied what had taken place or its equivalent. He was delighted. My observation is that almost everybody is by the verification of a prophecy, which he has made, or which he thinks he has made. Miss Spouter tried to laugh, but she didn't make much out of it. Mrs. Spouter didn't laugh at all. How could she when she remembered the plates of butter that had been consumed not only without thanks but without pay? She did all the talking in the domestic circle. Mr. Spouter seemed inclined to be taciturn. He merely remarked that he had never been so outed in his born days, and then shut up. But, then. Mr. Spouter never had much to say when Mrs. Spouter had the floor; If however, he had had the floor now, there was nothing for him to say. He had not sued his debtor but for reasons other than the being a merciful creditor. He was not used to such things. Indeed, the very word SUIT was, and had long been, disagreeable to his ear. So much so, that he had never gone into court of his own accord. It was one of his boasts, in comparing himself with some others, that he had never been plaintiff in an action, and never expected to be. He always discouraged people from going to law, maintaining that people never got much by going there, a remark that was true, when confined in its application to those who had gone there, carrying him with them. Yet, Mr. Spouter seldom lost a bill. It was always a wonder to me how rapidly persons in his condition could collect their bills. But this time Mr. Spouter, as he said, was outed. As he didn't relish Mr. Bill Williams' joke, and as Mrs. Spouter didn't, and at last, as Miss Spouter didn't, Mr. B. W. had to suspend.

Poor Mr. Pucket! his mind had been set upon a fee; but as no one could be found who could run faster than Mr. Triplet, and as the fugitive had gotten three days' start, there was no pursuit. None but a briefless lawyer can imagine how badly Mr. Pucket felt.

'And so she isn't married after all!' said Miss Spouter to herself, when she was alone in her chamber that night. 'Not married after all; no more than I am. Yes, I suppose more than I am, because she thought she was married, and I KNEW I wasn't. That makes some difference; and then—and then ——,' but it was too wonderful for Miss Spouter, she couldn't make it out. So she only said, 'Oh, I wonder how she feels!'

Now, there was but one way to get the desired information, and that was to see her and hear it from her own mouth. To most persons that way would seem to be barred, because the last time the two ladies met, Miss Spouter had refused to speak. But it did not seem so to her; she would herself remove all obstacles: SHE WOULD FORGIVE GEORGE! Yes, that she would. Wasn't it noble to forgive? Didn't the Bible teach us to forgive? Yes, she would forgive. What a glory overspread the heart of the injured when, in that tender moment, she found she could forgive. She wished now that she had gone to Georgiana to-day; she would go to-morrow. Malice should never have an abiding place in that heart. It might have it in other people's hearts, but it never should have it in that one. She laid herself calmly and sweetly upon her bed, and was forcibly reminded, as she thought of herself and her conduct, of the beauty and the serenity of a summer's evening.

CHAPTER VII.

"In that same place thou hast appointed me
To-morrow truly will I meet with thee."
                              Midsummer Night's Dream.

Mr. Pea writhed and chafed under his oath. He begged his Georgy to let him tell somebody. He swore another oath that he should die if he didn't. He did tell it there in the house several times to imaginary auditors, after looking out of the doors and windows to see if no real ones were near. Even when he was out of doors, he went all about whispering excitedly to himself, occasionally laughing most tumultuously. Georgiana became uneasy.

'Pap, are you going to run distracted again ?'

'Georgy, ef I don't believe I am I'll—— you may kill me.'

Georgiana had to yield. She wished to see Mr. Spouter upon a little matter of business connected with Mr. Slack, and she concluded to consent for him to be sent for and her father to inform him of what she saw he must inevitably tell somebody. The old man was extremely thankful, but he wanted to make a request.

'Georgy, you must let me send for Triplet. I've got a good joke on Triplet, a powerful joke on him. And he's a officer, Georgy, too,' he added, seriously.

'Triplet is a officer. This case, an' a leetle more, an' it would a got into cote; an' as Triplet ar' a officer, he ought to be here in cose.'

Georgiana consented on hearing this last argument. But she expressly enjoined upon her father, that at any period of his disclosures, when she called upon him to stop, he had to do it. He promised to obey, and the servant was sent into Dukesborough with the request that Messrs. Spouter & Triplet should come out the next morning on particular business. Georgiana knew fully what she, who was her friend but now, alas, abandoned, was thinking about, and therefore she was included in the summons.

Early the next morning the party arrived. Miss Spouter alighted in great agitation, rushed through the front room into Georgiana's who was there waiting for what she knew was to happen, looked all around as if she was expecting to find somebody besides Georgiana, fell upon her in the old way pronounced her pardon, and then demanded to be told all about it. Oh, my! Dreadful! Did ever! Vain and foolish man ! How did Georgiana feel !

Georgiana led her into her father's room, which also served for the parlor. She was surprised and annoyed to find Mr. Pucket there with the other gentlemen. Mr. Pucket had, somehow, gotten the wind of it, and said to himself that he didn't know what might happen. He had been told by an old lawyer that the only way for a young man to succeed at the bar was to push himself forward. So he determined to go, and he went. Uncle Ben was glad of it. He was going, for the first time in his life, to make a speech, and he wished as large an audience as possible. No, no; in case there wern't no intrusion, and no nothin of the sort, nor nothin else.

Georgiana sat very near her father.

Then he opened his mouth and began :

'You see, gentul-men, it was all my fault, from the fust. After Georgy seed him she didn't think much of him. She said she didn't keer about marryin no how, and ef she did, she wanted it to be to a Southering man. But I

and him too, we overpersuaded her. He seemed to think so much of me and
her too; and he had a store, and 'peared like a man well to do. And I did
want to see my only daughter settle herself. The feelin is nat'ral, as you know
yourself, Mr. Spouter: all parrents that has daughters, has 'em, ain't it so,
Mr. Spouter?'

Mr. Spouter answered rather by his manner than in words. Miss Spouter
became confused, and didn't look at Mr. Pucket when he coughed, although
he was a married man. Mr. Triplet had seen somewhat of life in his time—
still he took a chew of t bacco.

'Go on, pap,' said Georgiana.

'Yes; well, you see, gentulmen, sich it war—any how they got married.
Georgy said when she gin her consent, she gin it to keep me from runnin distracted, as it did 'pear like I war. Howbeever, I ar clean out o' that now.
Circumances is altered powerful. Well, as I said, any how they got married
—that is, they didn't git married, because he were already married and thay
warn't no law for it, as you know yourself, Mr. Pucket, they warn't. But—
ah—leastways they went throo the—ah—the motions and the—ah—gittin out,
lisens, and the—ah—stannin up in the floor and jinin o' hands, and he come
here to live. Well now, don't you b'leeve that Georgy, she spishoned him
from the very fust day: for no sooner were he married hardly, than he began
to reach behind every nuke and corner about here, and before night, bless your
soul, he knowed more about whar things was in this house than I did. Leastways, Georgy says so, and its obleeged to be so; for there's things, many of
'em in this house that I don't know whar thay are.' And Mr. Pea looked
around and above, taking as big a view as if he were surveying the whole
uni verse.

'Well, Georgy, she and he tuk a walk that fust evenin. Instid of talkin
along like tother folks that's jest got married, he went right straight to talkin
about settlin hisself, and put at her to begin right away to git all she could
out'n me; which, Georgy, she didn't like no sich, and no body wouldn't a
liked it that thought anything of herself. You wouldn't, Angeline Spouter,
you know you wouldn't, the very fust day you was married.'

'Go on, pap, please.'

'Yes, well, Georgy spishuned him agin at supper, from the way he looked
at the spoons on the table; which ef they had a been the genuine silver, they
wouldnt a been in this house now, to my opinion, probly, leastways, ef——,
uncle Ben smiled and concluded to postpone the balance of this sentence.

'Well, you see, Georgy Ann, arter supper, she got sick, she did, and she
hilt on to her head powerful. In coce bed time, hit had to come arter a while,

when hit did come, she were wusser, and she give that feller a candle to go
long to bed by hisself. When she went to bed, I thought she was a goin on
in thar in cose, like 'tother married people; but she, instid o' that, she went
on thoo into the little jinin back room and she locked the door arter her. I
never knowed one word o' this untel arter he went off. Well, arter he went
to sleep, Georgy, she heered a mighty groanin. So she ups, she does, an
onlocks the door and creeps in mighty sly. It seem like he ware dreaming
and talkin in his sleep powerful. He called names, sich as Jemimy, Susan
Jane, Betsy Ann, and—what was all them names, Georgy?'

'It makes no difierence, pap, go on.'

'And a heap more of 'em. Georgy can tell you. Cose she heard 'em over
and ofting. Well, he seemed to be powerful shamed of all of 'em, and he swore
he wern't married and them that said so was a liar, and all sich. Well, sich
catrin on made Georgy b'leve that he was a married man befo, and had two
or three wives already, or probable four or five. And so she jist wouldn't
sleep with him no how. She—well, in fac, she jist didn't think she was
liable too sleep with him. And she was right, Triplet, she was right, wasn't
she Triplet?'

'In cose,' answered Mr. Triplet.

'Do go on, pap.'

'Well, yes. Yit still she didn't let on. She kep up tolerable well in the
day time, but when night come, Georgy she kep on gittin sick, and goin into
the jinin little room. I never seed sich carrin on befo.'

Uncle Ben would stop and laugh some. Georgy begged him to go on.

'Well, she kep on hearin him a goin on, and you think she would tell me
the fust thing o' all this. Ef she had a told me, howbeever, that aint neither
here nor thar. Well, it seem he talked in his sleep about other people besides wimming, about men and about money, and declared on his soul that he
never stole it, which goes to show Georgy that he war a rogue as well as a
rascal about winning. Yit in this time he begin to hint even around me
about property, and even insinivated that he would like to have the whole
plantation and all that's on it.' Mr. Pea showed plainly by his manner, after
making this last remark, that no man had ever had an ambition more boundless than the late Mr. Slack.

'But I mighty soon give him to understand that he war barkin up the
wrong tree ef he thought. I was gwine to give up this plantation and my
property before my head got cold. Men's always fools that does it.'

'Howbeever, he talked so much about settlin hisself, and so easy and good
about Georgy, and how that all he keered about property war her, and I

knowed that was all I keered about it for, that I told him, I'd pay for a nigger 'oman for 'em. Well, you see, I no sooner says that than he ups with a lie about havin to go to Augusty. But shore enuff, arter he had been here two or three days, he had to go too Augusty, or somewhar else. Becase he got a letter which skeered him powerful, an he said he war gwine right off. I didn't spishun nothin agin the man, and I lets him have the money to buy the nigger 'oman. I had no more spishun of him, deems Triplet, than I have of you, only knowin that he was monstrous fond of money, which is all right enough, ef a man comes by it honest. Well, Georgy she was tuk back tremenduous by his gittin the money so all on a sudding. Yit she didn't let on, but makes out like she's mighty sorry he war goin so soon, but mighty glad he's goin to fetch her a nigger 'oman when he come back. She has him got a mighty good smack of vittles, and what ain't common for dinner, she puts on the table a plate of nice fresh butter and a plenty of biscuit, Triplet,' Mr. Pea now looked as sly and as good humored as it was possible for him to be. 'Triplet, I've got a good joke on you.'

Mr. Triplet seemed to guess what it was, and smiled subduedly.

'You know what you said about my never seein certing peeple and certing things—certing property no more?'

Mr. Triplet acknowledged that he did.

'Well, Triplet, part of it was so and part of it were not so, all which both is jist as I wants it to be. Triplet, that butter and them biscuit is what saved me. He never expected to eat no more tell he got to Augusty, and I tell you he hung to that butter and them biscuit. While he was at 'em, and Georgy she made 'em late a comin in a purpose, she takes some old keys which she had picked up, and finds one that could onlock his pelcese whar she seed him put the money, and whar she knowed he kep all he had.'

Uncle Ben intended to laugh mercilessly at Triplet, but he was stopped by the sight of Mr. Pucket, who did as if he was trying to swallow something that was too big for his throat.

'Ar anything the matter with you Mr. Pucket? Is you got a cold?' Ar your thoat so?' asked the old gentleman, with undisguised interest:

Triplet snickered as Mr. Pucket denied being sick,

Uncle Ben proceeded:

'So she jest opened it sly as a mice and took out my money—'

'And what else?' eagerly asked Mr. Pucket.

'My watch, that the villion beg me to let him take with him to have it worked on, which I didn't like no——'

'What else?' asked Mr. Pucket again.

'That's the last pint I'm a comin too, and that's why Georgy sent arter Mr. Spouter. She knowed that he owed Mr. Spouter thirry dollars, and she made up her mind to pay the debt as now she seed his money, and she tuck out thirty dollars o' his money, which here it ar for you Mr. Spouter.'

'I garnishee the thirty dollars,' interposed Mr. Pucket, holding out his hands.

'You are too late,' answered Mr. Spouter, taking the money, putting it into his pocket, and looking as if he had gotten in again after being ousted by Mr. Slack.

'Can't I garnishee, Triplet?''

'Garnishee for what?'

'For my fee?'

'Fee for what?'

'Why, for my services in —ah,— coming out here on two occasions.'

'Well you can't garnishee.'

Mr. Triplet looked as if he was ashamed of Mr. Pucket. Uncle Ben hoped there was goin' to be no bad feelins, and no difficulties.

'Certainly not,' answered Mr. Triplet. 'Mr. Pucket ar' a young lawyer, and forgot at the minit that it war other people that owed him for his services in stid of Mr. Slack: Besides, furthermo, Mr. Pucket ought to know that you can't garnishee jist dry so, without fust gittin' out some sort o' paper from the cote. That would take so much time that Spouter, here, mout spend his thirty dollars befo he got it, that is, ef Spouter wanted too.' Mr. Triplet looked interrogatingly at the 'tother gentleman.

'Yes, ef I wanted too,' answered Mr: S., oraculously:

'But,' persisted Mr. Pucket, 'there was other monies.'

'Whar?' asked Mr. Triplet.

'In Mr. Slack's trunk.'

'No they want,' answered Mr. Pea, who thought he ought to keep Mr. Pucket to the true word. 'They was in his pelease.'

'Well, in his pelease. That makes no difference,' and Mr. Pucket looked as if he thought he had them on that point.

'Pucket,' said Triplet, 'it won't make no difference. You are right. It don't make nary bit o' difference with no body, nor with your fee neither. That fee ar' a lost ball. They aint no money here to pay it with, an' ef there was, it would be Mr. Slack's lawyer, and not you that would git it. Well, gin it up and another time try to have better luck.'

Mr. Pucket *was* a young lawyer, and was, in part, owned by Mr. Triplet. So he subsided. Uncle Ben looked troubled, until the sheriff assured him that there could be no difficulties. 'Go on, uncle Ben. You got your gun, of cours?'

'Triplet, you rascal'! You may laugh; but I don't want the gun. He may keep it, and do what he pleases with it, even to blowin' out his own thevious brains with it for what I keer. He's welcome to the gun. You Triplet!'

'Don't mind me, uncle Ben. Go on.'

'Well, thar's lots more to tell ef Georgy would only let me; and some things as would make you laugh powerful, Triplet, ef you was to hear 'em. But she's made me swar, actily swar, that I won't tell without her leave. Maybe she'll tell your ole 'oman some o' these days. Well, I felt mighty glad when I got my money back, and, ef any thing, a wosser gladder when I got back my watch agin. Triplet, when I seed her,' (and the old man drew out a watch as big and as round as a turnip.) 'when I seed her agin, ef I didn't cry you may kill me. I've had her thirty year, and none o' your new-fangled ones can beat her runnin' when you clean her out and keep her sot right with the sun. Ah, well, he continued, putting it back and staking his foot in mild satisfaction; 'the thing is over, and the best of it all ar' that ——'

'Hush pap,' said Georgiana, raising her finger.

The old man smiled and hushed.

After hearing parts of the story over several times, the party rose to go. Mr. Triplet rising, said that in case it war not any of his bisiness but he would like to ax Miss Georgy one question, of he wouldn't be considered as meddlin' with what didn't belong to him; and that was why she didn't tell on the villion as soon as she found him out. Georgiana answered:

'Well, Mr. Triplet, I many times thought I would; but she seed did'nt know for certain that he had done all the things that I was afraid be had. Besides, Mr. Triplet, even if he was'nt my husband, I one time thought he was; and before God and man, I had promised to be faithful to him. And then he had staid in this house, and eat at our table, and—and called pap father, and—and—and— Well, Mr. Triplet, somehow. it didn't look right for me to be the first one to turn against him; and—and when I did think of telling on him. something would rise up and tell me that I ought not.'

'Wimming aint like men no how, uncle B n,' said Triplet. wiping his eye as he bade him good bye.

'No they aint, Triplet,' and he laid his and fondly on his daughter's shoulder while the tears ran down his checks.

The visitors now left, all except Miss Spouter. She wished to get behind the scenes and know more. How much more she learned I cannot say. They went to bed early when the day ended, and to sleep late. There was something which made them easily reunite. It was a pity. Miss Spouter imagined that she pitied her friend because she had been deceived by a man, even more than herself had ever been, and because of the hurtful influence which that deception would probably exert upon any future expectations of marriage. Miss Pea, who, instead of having any regrets, felt relief in the thought that henceforth her father would be satisfied to allow her to manage such matters for herself, and that she should be satisfied to have none to manage, really pitied her friend because she yet yearned for an impossible estate. When the time came for them to go to sleep, (and Georgiana thought it long coming) she did not wait a moment. Miss Spouter lay awake some time further. She pondered long on what she had heard. It was strange. It was almost like a novel. How could George be still the same Georgiana Pea? She had been Mrs. Slack. Wasn't she Mrs. Slack now; and how, oh ! how exciting everything must have been. Her thoughts followed Mr. Slack a while; but he was so far away that they came back and went looking after Mr. Bill Williams. He was not much, but he was something. He had never exhibited any regard for her yet, but it was possible that he would some day. He was at least ten years younger than herself. But her curls were the same as ever, and besides. were not marriages made in Heaven? or were they not a lottery, or something of the sort? Who knows? Mr. Bill Williams, after all, might be the very one to whom the something in her alluded when it had so repeatedly told her that she was destined to make some man so happy. Then her mind turned again, and notwithstanding Mr. Slack's great distance ahead, it started forth in the direction he had taken. She dwelt upon his strange conduct and his running away, and although it was plain that he had done the like before, and when he had never seen her nor heard of her, yet, she halfway persuaded herself that she was the cause, though the perfectly innocent cause, of it all. Yes, yes l' she was saying to herself, as sleep stole upon her at last, 'he is one, but the image of Angeline Spouter is in his breast, and it will stay there